VENOMOUS TIDINGS

AN ACADEMY OBSCURA HOLIDAY STORY

CASSIA BRIAR

Wednesday Ink

VENOMOUS TIDINGS

Cover by Crooked Sixpence Book Covers

Editing by Sinful Aloha

*Monsters and Christmas,
what could go wrong?*

CONTENTS

CONTENT INFORMATION

If you don't like TWs then please skip this page!

This book contains, but is not limited to, dark themes, primal chasing, violence, revenge, language, death, murder, bullying, dark thoughts, and other potentially triggering situations. Your mental health matters, please read responsibly.

CHARM

"**C**harm." His deep, seductive voice purred into my ear. Warmth washed over me, my body hummed and tingled like a live wire. I moaned in anticipation of what was to come.

Every night he, and the others, visited my dreams. My nighttime world was consumed by them. Their rough skin glided across mine, their whispers filled my mind, and they used their bodies to pleasure me.

"One day we'll come for you, Charm."

Every night he made the same promise before his forked tongue teased my nipples, then flicked over my bare stomach all the way down to my pulsating clit. The other creature palmed my breasts, as the third watched us.

For some reason, I was always naked in these dreams. Naked and horny. They made me feel so good that I didn't care about the fact that I never saw their faces. Never *clearly saw their forms either. I wasn't sure what kind of beings they were, only that they weren't human.*

I writhed as he tormented me with his long tongue and sharp, deadly fangs. My focus was mostly on the two dream-creatures who pleasured me in this strange, mist-shrouded place. Whenever I glanced beyond them, I was met with impenetrable darkness. An inky black that sometimes gazed back with glowing yellow eyes. I'd blink, and they'd vanish. So strange.

But that was how I knew there was a third one who watched us from afar. He never spoke, and never engaged. However, his heated gaze turned me on. I enjoyed putting on a show for him with the others.

I drew in a sharp breath, then released it on a moan as one of them filled me with three thick fingers. They pumped in and out of me.

"So wet for us," he murmured. "Come for me, Charm."

His wicked tongue lapped at my clit, while the other pinched my nipples, and I shattered into a million tiny pieces.

With a gasp, I woke up in my bed. The deep gray of a winter's dawn told me it was chilly outside, but I was burning up. My skin felt too hot and tight. The silk camisole clung to my clammy flesh, and my panties were drenched. It happened every single night.

"That fucking dream," I muttered, tossing the tangled covers aside. I stretched as I made my way to the bathroom for a much-needed shower.

Turning on the spray, I stepped into the steaming water.

Why did I keep having the same dream night after night? I thought back to when they started. Almost exactly a year ago. Which meant a few weeks after both of my parents were murdered. My chest pinched with grief. I missed them so much and this was going to be a hard Yule—my first holiday season without them in my life.

Because of that, I was staying on campus this year. Since their deaths, I was alone in this world. My heart pinched. Grief settled over me like a shroud.

I touched the charm bracelet that I'd worn since my mother gave it to me for safe-keeping. My only remaining connection to them. It was a family heirloom and a constant reminder of my parents. And how I was on my own now.

My eyes burned, and I blinked away the sensation. Sheesh. Maybe I needed to adopt a cat or something, because even to myself, I sounded kind of pathetic. Lonely. Almost a year later, and the gaping wound in my heart hadn't healed yet. Would it ever? I guess grief processed in its own time, there was no point in trying to rush it, no matter how miserable I was every day.

At least my dream-time monsters kept me company at night. I didn't know how else to describe them because they certainly weren't human or any type of supernatural I'd ever met. Long tongues, rough touches, and that seductive tone of the one who spoke —that was all I knew of them. The dark hid their features. Even so, I'd become comfortable with them. Their presence soothed me.

They gave me pleasure that was more than physical in my dreams. We talked about life sometimes, too. About my family, all of my sorrows, hopes, and dreams for the future. Every night when I went to bed, I was entering my safe space. Almost like an alternate reality where I could simply be me without judgement.

It was my haven.

That sounded totally delusional, but it was better than talking to a therapist on campus. At least the creatures in my dreams believed me when I told them who murdered my parents. My shrink had never said it aloud, but I knew she thought I was making things up. That's why I stopped seeing her several months ago. I couldn't stand another moment of her quiet judgment or that fake smile.

Finishing up, I grabbed a white fluffy towel and dried off. I wrapped my hair in a thinner towel, then chose my outfit for the day.

I dressed in dark jeans, a cerulean blue sweater that matched my eyes, and tall black boots. After drying my straight dark hair, I gave myself a once over in the full-length mirror. *Not too shabby.*

Not that I was likely to run into very many people today. Campus had been pretty much deserted since the beginning of winter break, and it would remain that way until after the New Year.

In the small kitchen that occupied one corner of my modest, studio apartment, I scavenged for breakfast. A wasted effort. I came up with a near empty carton of Oreo ice cream and a moldy banana. I sighed.

Tossing the banana in the trash, I spooned out the remainder of the ice cream.

The great thing about being an adult? You could eat ice cream whenever you wanted, even for breakfast.

As I spooned out the yummy frozen confection, I considered my options for the day. I could go to my office and get a start on cleaning it up and organizing for next term... Nah, where was the fun in that? I was technically on vacation. I suppose I could—

My cell pinged with a new text message. I snatched it off the nightstand and frowned when I saw it was from Dean Wright. She wanted me to come to her office as soon as possible. Obviously, she didn't believe in vacations.

I licked the remaining ice cream from my spoon, feeling woefully unsatisfied by the meager breakfast. I'd find something more nutritional after seeing the dean.

Grabbing my snowflake obsidian wand and stashing it in my pocket, I left my apartment in Academy Hall and hurried through the frigid morning air to the Dean's Hall.

Academy Obscura was unusually quiet, and the deserted atmosphere of the place hung heavily around me. Even the creatures who were out and about in the winter seemed subdued today. My gut twisted with unease.

I pushed through the doors to the Dean's Hall and the disquiet vanished—mostly. A huge, decorated tree stood in the middle of the lobby. Enchanted snow fell from the vaulted ceiling onto the floor around it. A couple of professors sat by the fireplace. The sweet scent of hot cocoa and sugar cookies made my mouth water and my stomach grumble. I swiped two cookies from the table.

"Good morning, Miss Beaumont," said Professor Till, momentarily breaking from his conversation with our new Potions teacher. "How is my best assistant doing today?"

I gave him a slight grin. I was his only assistant this year, having taken the job right after graduation, and I doubted I was any better than those who'd come before me. Even so, Professor Till handed out compliments like they were Halloween candy. It was one of the things I liked most about him. Feeling down and in need of a boost? Just spend ten minutes with our Charms teacher.

Did I find it laughable that my name was Charm and I assisted the Magical Charms teacher? Yes. So did most of the students. In fact, I never heard the end of it.

"Good morning." I smiled at both professors. "I'm good. The dean wants to see me in her office." I used my remaining cookie to point up the staircase. "Gotta go."

Professor Till waved me off. "When you're done,

come back down and have a taste of this year's Green Witch Brew. It's my best yet!"

With a wave, I sprinted up the stairs to hide my disgusted expression. Professor Till was famous for his take on absinthe. He turned the Green Fairy into the Green Witch, and boy was she a spiteful old hag.

Last Yule, a bunch of seniors swiped a bottle from his office—yes, I was among them. The hangover from drinking that stuff was brutal. I thought my brain was going to melt right out of my eye sockets.

Never. Again.

I knocked on the dean's solid wooden door.

"Come in!" Dean Wright called.

I slipped inside, and strode toward her massive desk. Her purple hair framed her face as she pored over a letter, motioning me forward with one hand.

Dean Wright had been in charge of Academy Obscura since before the revolution almost thirty years ago. The academy may have changed from a two-year school to a four-year university, and the world around us may have altered, but somehow the dean hadn't aged a day.

I'd seen pictures of her with the queen from back then. Honestly, the woman seemed to be immortal. Which she wasn't, of course, but I needed the inside scoop on her skin care routine. It wasn't only Fae magic that kept her so preserved, I was sure of it.

"Charm," she said my name, and I realized I'd been openly staring at her flawless pores.

"Yeah?"

"You're hovering. Sit down, please." Amusement briefly curled the corners of her lips.

I did as she asked, then waited. Hands folded in my lap.

Dean Wright picked up the letter on her desk, and her smile disappeared. "I'm afraid I have some disturbing news. I'm sorry."

When she didn't immediately spit it out, I leaned forward slightly in my chair. My mind raced with what kind of bad news could possibly involve me. I had no family. I was pretty sure my position here as a teacher's aide was secure. Unless the news was about...

She let the letter drop from her fingers. "They didn't have enough to hold him after the investigation concluded last week." Dean Wright heaved a heavy sigh. "Sander La Croix has been set free from Grimsmore Prison and all charges have been dropped."

My stomach squeezed into a tight ball. I gaped at her. The authorities had released the man who'd murdered my parents?

"How could that happen?" I demanded, a jolt of outrage sparked through me. "What more evidence do they need? I *saw* him leaving my parents' house."

"But you didn't see him commit the crime." Her soft smile held sympathy.

"It was him! They have his wand. They know it was

magic that killed them." I grunted in frustration. "How could they let him go? This is terrible." Slumping in my seat, I ran my fingers through my hair. This was a disaster.

"I'm sorry to say that it gets worse." She winced at my startled expression.

"How could it possibly get worse?" I asked, immediately regretting my words. *Great way to jinx yourself, Charm.*

"Mr. La Croix has requested, and been granted by the Council, a teaching position here starting next term. He is due to arrive in a couple of days. I'm sorry. There was nothing I could do about it." Regret shone in her eyes.

"He's coming *here*?" I stood so abruptly that the chair tipped over and crashed to the floor.

She nodded. "This teaching position is part of the restitution for keeping an innocent man in prison for a year."

"He's *not* innocent," I snarled. My palms smacked against her desk top. "This is ridiculous!"

"Whether innocent or guilty, he's been cleared of all charges. I'm really sorry."

"You don't need to be sorry," I said, "but *he* will be. Mark my words." Spinning on my heel, I marched toward the door.

"Miss Beaumont— *Charm*, don't do anything you might regret."

I turned to face her. "Don't worry about me. I won't regret a thing."

"I mean it, Charm. If you stir up trouble with Mr. La Croix, I might be forced to remove you from your position here." She was caught in the middle, I knew that, but her words still stung. The threat was clear. I had to play nice, or else I could literally lose everything.

For a moment I blinked at her, unable to form words. She couldn't take away my teaching assistant position. It was all I had left. I let that reality sink in for a minute.

There was no future in which I would let that happen.

"*Me* stir up trouble?" I finally said. "Why do you think La Croix specifically asked to teach *here*? Where I am. He could have chosen any other academy."

"You know what I mean." She sighed. "But this is neither the time nor place for revenge. I'm sorry. I'll be sure to stress the same point with Mr. La Croix when he arrives. There will be no bloodshed at this academy. Am I clear?"

I can't promise that.

I gave a curt nod. Rage blinded me as I left her office and stormed down the stairs. The lobby was empty, and for several seconds, I just stood there, seething. How could this be happening? Grief, disbelief, and fear mingled with my anger, until I felt dizzy.

La Croix murdered my parents. I knew he did. Now he was on his way here to finish the job.

Out of the corner of my eye, I spotted a familiar bright green bottle with a black and orange label on it:

Green Witch Brew. I only hesitated a second before snatching it up and rushing back to my apartment in Academy Hall.

This was a very, very bad idea. But I needed something to dull the pain and rage.

CHARM

By the time the bottle was half empty, my head felt fuzzy, and I had to squint to see clearly across my single room apartment. But the booze had done its job and my emotions were as numb as they were going to get. My raging anger had died down to a dull ache in my chest.

I toyed with the charm bracelet around my wrist. Mom had given it to me for safe-keeping mere weeks before she and Dad were murdered. Besides it being a family heirloom, I didn't know much about the piece of jewelry.

Studying it closer, I fingered the individual small charms. Every other one was a different type of snake. One had black scales, another blue-green, and then crimson. Between them were magical symbols. A star, a crescent moon, and an Egyptian Ankh. An infinity figure eight held the clasp.

What did they mean?

Curious, I pulled out my snowflake obsidian wand and pointed it at my wrist. "Reveal your purpose," I slurred. A tiny puff of peachy magic escaped the end of my wand and coated the charms, tickling my skin.

I waited, but nothing happened. "Well, shit. That was a pointless waste of magic."

Thinking, I waved my wand like an orchestra conductor until inspiration struck. I came up with a long string of Latin words and sang them out at the top of my lungs. Much like a Christmas carol, though certainly off key.

To my surprise, the bracelet warmed as tiny fiery bits of magic burst from my wand.

I giggled at the glittery sparkles that reminded me of tinsel. "Now that's some holiday cheer, right there."

Were *cheer* and *there* supposed to rhyme? *Cheer... Theer..?*

My musings were cut short as a blinding light split the air in the middle of my apartment. Literally, it was like a tear in what should have been open floor space.

To my horror, and amusement, the light widened and expanded until it formed a dark opening. It was like looking into a void.

Whoa.

I leaned forward and lost my balance. With a squeak, I fell off the bed. Since I was already down here, I decided to crouch on the floor. Seemed much easier than trying to stand on my unsteady legs.

Crap, there's a void in my apartment. What should I do?

I knew drinking this much Green Witch Brew was a bad idea, but this? This was next level. I'd conjured a portal or something. Until I investigated, I wouldn't know what it was.

I edged toward the foot of my bed to get a better look.

"Where is she?" a deep, familiar voice asked.

I froze.

Shaking my head, I tried to clear it because I'd only ever heard *his* voice when I was asleep. Was I dreaming right now? Because that would explain a lot.

I pinched myself. *Ouch*. Why did I have to do that so hard?

No, not dreaming. Which meant this was reality. Or maybe a booze-induced hallucination?

"Maybe she left," an even deeper voice rumbled.

There's more than one of them.

The familiar male spoke again. "No, I can smell her. She's here."

Smell me? I peeked over the edge of my mattress just in time to see the speaker's forked tongue flick out and taste the air.

I blinked—hard—several times. But the apparitions remained.

There were three of them. Either that or I was having triple vision. Blinking again, I tried to clear my head. Nope, still three of them standing on the other side of my bed, in front of that gaping hole in space.

They weren't men, that was for sure. Their skin was tattooed in patterns that resembled a snake's markings. Add to that, slitted pupils, forked tongues, and one of them had huge horns…

Yeah, *hell no. No way am I sticking around for whatever comes next.*

Worst of all? They were looking for *me*. Why?

Better to not stick around a find out.

I stood, and bolted out the door, miraculously managing to not trip over myself as I fled. My fluffy sock-clad feet pounded the stone floor and stairs as I sprinted down to the building's exit. I didn't have a destination in mind; I just ran like I was being chased by demons. Snake demons.

A quick glance over my shoulder confirmed as much. *Oh shit.*

They were shouting at me, but I couldn't make sense of their words. Their meaning drowned out by the whoosh of blood rushing in my ears. My heart beat so fast, I was afraid it might tear through my ribcage. But absolutely nothing was going to slow me down.

I body-slammed the heavy wooden front doors, then was suddenly outside in the chilly rain-drenched night. The damp air helped to clear my head a bit. I needed to get help.

How was I going to explain these creatures to the dean? No idea. I wasn't even sure where they came from, only that I had to escape them.

I took off for the dense forest behind Academy Hall. My socks instantly grew soggy. Icy rain soaked my hair and clothing in seconds, plastering both to my chilled skin. The fog was so thick I could barely see a foot in any direction, but I sensed those monsters on my tail.

So I ran even harder, faster.

A pine branch whacked me in the face, and I was momentarily blinded. *Ouch!*

My shin caught on a log, and I went down with a yelp of pain.

Spitting damp earth, pine needles, and moss out of my mouth, I sat up with a groan and reached for my wand. Coming up empty-handed, I realized I'd left it in my apartment. I was unarmed out in the frigid night, in the near dark, and being hunted.

Nice, Charm, real smart move.

I quickly got to my feet and my head swam. The foggy world around me tilted. I fought against the temptation to move with it.

A twig snapped. I spun around just as a massive body came down on mine. We hit the ground with a loud thunk.

My heart hammered against my ribs. I couldn't breathe. Fear drove all rational thought from my mind.

Run? Already tried that.

Fight? Definitely not.

Play dead? Good idea.

His heavy body pressed down on mine. "Charm," his deep voice purred against my ear, "I promised we'd come for you."

CHARM

My entire body stilled, even my heart stopped beating for several seconds. This couldn't be happening. How was my dream-lover made real? Every fiber of my being recognized him, and realized the truth instantly.

My skin prickled and warmed in anticipation of what his bare flesh would feel like against me, of him inside of me, of being lost in his touch.

I drew in a ragged breath. My pussy clenched with need.

Had someone granted my Yuletide wish early? Because if I were being honest, I had desperately wanted to meet my dream-lovers in the flesh. Now, *poof*, here was one of them lying on top of me as it rained down on us.

My fear receded, replaced with curiosity. Then I glanced around his shoulder and spotted the other two demons standing close, their eyes glowing yellow in the fog.

Holy shit, holy shit, they're real, too.

And all three of them were monsters. Huge, tattooed, and demonic. Not exactly what I was expecting them to look like. I swallowed hard, a fresh wave of fear rippled through my veins.

"Are you hurt?" asked the demon I was clinging to on the ground. At this point, I used his body to shield myself from the others. All of their attention on me was too intense. Too much to take all at once.

I inhaled deeply, breathing in his familiar ocean air scent. That did wonders to both help clear my head and calm my nerves.

"Who are you?" I asked, just to make sure I wasn't delusional. What if they weren't who I assumed they were?

"My name is Drake." He scooped me into his arms and stood, facing the other two. I clung to him like flock on a tree. "That is Arik and Ty. Now you have our names, love."

Their illuminated, slitted eyes shone in the darkness. Eeriness settled over me. I said nothing, and let Drake carry me back to my apartment.

My drunk brain raced with a thousand questions. I held off asking anything until I'd changed out of my wet clothes and emerged from the bathroom, half expecting them to have vanished.

Surprisingly, the three demons were still there.

I stumbled over to the sofa, and not so gracefully

tripped on the corner of it. Drake caught me in his arms before I could bash my head on the coffee table.

Ugh, stupid drunk witch. The hangover tomorrow was going to be epic.

"I smell poison in your blood," said Drake, raking his nose along my jawline and making me shiver.

A sudden giggle burst from my lips. "You call it poison. We call it booze."

"I can fix this for you." Without warning, Drake's canines elongated into deadly fangs, which he sank into the side of my neck.

I shrieked. Pain, surprise, and desire tangled in my gut.

He held me against him, ignored my flailing, and drank like a vampire. What the hell? Numb tingling turned into a full sensation in my body, and gradually my mind cleared.

In moments, I was sober as could be. *Damn it.* Although now I didn't have to worry about that hangover.

Drake eased back, his fangs retracting, and I gazed at him, really seeing him for the first time—with all my senses intact.

A symmetrical pattern in blues and greens covered his skin, making me think of the sea. His slitted pupils were black, surrounded by a deep cobalt. Dark brown waves of damp hair stuck up at odd angles. He was equally alluring and terrifying.

"Thanks," I murmured.

Straightening up, I took a step back and dragged

my attention away from him. I glanced at the other two. Arik was a giant red-head with deep crimson and orange markings on his creamy skin. His bright green eyes surveyed me with open interest.

The third one, Ty, had short, straight black hair and curved horns. Black and gray marked his deeply tanned complexion. His hazel gaze narrowed as I took him in, immediately sending warning bells ringing through my mind. Of the three of them, he reminded me the most of a deadly viper waiting to strike. I'd certainly keep my distance from him.

Was he the one who watched? Heat spread across my cheeks. It didn't matter.

I returned my attention to Drake. "What are you exactly, and where did you come from? How are you *here?*"

He gracefully lounged on the couch, while the other two stood across the room watching us. Their massive arms folded. "As you may have guessed, we're demons. Snake demons, to be exact. And we came from the Underworld through the portal you opened."

A portal to the Underworld… Was that what the light in the middle of my apartment had been? It was gone when we returned. I seriously thought I'd hallucinated that part. How the fuck had I opened a portal? Honestly, it was all kind of a blur.

I glanced at the three of them dressed in jeans and hoodies. "They have clothes in the Underworld?"

"No, we all just run around naked down there while carrying pitchforks," Drake deadpanned.

Okay, obviously he was joking. Right? Right. There were normal clothes in the Underworld. Noted.

I wrapped my arms around my middle and asked, "Why are you here?"

Drake's lush lips turned up at the corners. "You summoned us. We're here to grant your Yuletide wish, Charm."

My jaw dropped. Were they really here to give me a hundred orgasms? Let's be honest, it was slim pickings on campus. I'd graduated so recently that the idea of having sex with a teacher was kinda gross; yet getting it on with a senior was also unappealing since they were students. So, I was trapped in the middle. I hadn't had actual, *physical* sex with another person in over a year! Sexy snake demon-filled dreams didn't count.

Just to make sure we were on the same page, because Ty certainly didn't look thrilled about what Drake had said, I asked, "Which Yuletide wish would that be?"

Drake, who seemed to be their leader, smiled. "Vengeance. We're here to kill Sander La Croix and avenge your parents."

Well, that was a libido killer.

Charm was much smaller, and more fragile looking, in the flesh. Though no less intriguing. I liked the feel of her gaze raking over my face and body, and the way her cheeks turned pink. Her pretty blue eyes shifted and changed with her emotions. She was so very animated.

"Vengeance for my parents," she echoed my words.

I inclined my head. "That is your greatest wish, is it not?"

"One of them," she muttered, flushing a pretty deep pink. "Yes, yes it is."

My cock grew hard as I gazed at her. We'd spent almost a year in the dream world, not quite her realm and certainly not ours, an in-between. Where we all were also less than solid. Now that we were all on the same plane, I couldn't wait to really hear Charm's moans, to taste her, to feel her.

But I didn't dare move too fast. The last thing I wanted to do was scare our Charmer. And if I showed her everything I wanted to do to her right here, right now, she'd run away. Again.

Though I must admit, chasing my sweet girl through the woods was its own kind of fun. Did she feel it too? The rush, the excitement, the anticipation?

"So, how are you going to avenge my family?" Charm asked.

"Leave that to us, love. All in good time. You'll see." In the meantime, there was so much to tell her, so much she needed to understand. Again, all in good time.

I glanced at Arik and Ty, both standing like stone carvings near the door. We were all in this together, we had a plan and we needed to stick to it. This was too important to fuck it up.

Don't overwhelm Charm.

Don't say or do anything to scare her away.

Patience. That was how we'd get what we came for.

And what did we come for? *Her*.

CHARM

❄

"**I** still don't know how I opened that portal." I yawned. It was the early hours of the morning, and we were still up talking. Well, Drake and I were talking. Arik and Ty stood like sentinels near the door, but they were listening to our conversation. I was sure of it.

Drake shrugged. "All I know is that you summoned us here. Obviously, a connection has been forming between us for some time across the realms." His heated gaze swept over my body.

I blushed. Yeah, a *connection* sure had been forming in my dreams. I mean, we did talk, it wasn't all sex.

"What do we do now?" I asked with another yawn, curled up on one side of the sofa.

"We wait. La Croix will arrive soon. Then we will make a plan." He eyed me. "For now, we should sleep."

I nodded, glancing around my single room apartment with a frown. Besides the couch we were sitting on, there was my bed. My bed, which was large enough for at least three people, took up most of the space. I could swear it was taunting me right now. Though I didn't choose it, the huge mattress had always been there.

Potential problem solved.

"You guys can take the bed. I'll be fine on the sofa—"

Ty spoke for the first time. "We might be a snake den, but we don't actually sleep together. I'm taking the couch." He strode toward the sofa and sat so close to me that I recoiled from his menacing gaze.

Quickly, I jumped off the couch. "Fine." *Asshole.*

It wasn't like I hadn't been in bed with Drake before; we'd just never slept together in a physical form—or clothed. Or really ever actually *slept*. It was fine. I could totally do this. Just sleep. With demons. In my bed.

My gaze traveled to Arik. He seemed to be the strong, silent type. Was he opposed to…

I cleared my throat. "Three of us can fit easily on the bed, if that's cool with you."

He gave a curt nod, and stalked over to the bed. Without ceremony, or any sense of modesty, he stripped off his clothes. I stared, mouth open, at his rippling muscles and taut ass. His unique orange and crimson markings appeared across every inch of his body.

Hot damn.

He climbed under the thick comforter, and I snapped my jaw shut.

Okay, then... Sleeping next to him will be totally not weird.

To distract myself from that thought, I went about my business. Drake watched with amusement dancing in his blue eyes as I used my wand to ignite the hearth fire, then douse the overhead lights, leaving the room washed in a flickering orange glow.

I eased into bed fully clothed. On the one hand, I felt totally awkward sleeping in my bed with two near strangers. On the other hand, I was horny as fuck and totally turned on by the idea. Which wasn't helped much by Drake slowly peeling off his hoodie, revealing impressive abs and a deep V that disappeared into his jeans.

My mouth watered as he climbed into bed, gently shoving me into the middle between these two enormous, and gorgeous demons.

Holy hotness.

Technically, opening a portal to the Underworld and summoning demons was not great. In fact, it was dangerous. Seriously frowned upon. But at that moment, I wasn't especially worried about it. I just needed to keep my wits about me, and I'd be fine.

Demons were known to... you know, lie, cheat, steal your soul after you foolishly made a bargain with them. I just had to be careful.

"Relax, Charm." Drake lay on his side, facing me. His long, forked tongue darted out to taste my skin, and I gasped. "We won't bite—at least not again tonight."

Was I supposed to believe that?

With one last lingering glance, he rolled over, quickly falling asleep on his back. On my other side, Arik's breathing was slow and even. The fire crackled.

After such a long, crazy day, my eyelids drooped.

That night, my dreams were empty.

Late morning sunlight had broken through the cloud cover to shine upon campus. The three snake demons and I walked toward the dean's office. We'd been summoned. Apparently, someone had seen us last night and word had gotten back to the dean. Our story was all ironed out. So, I wasn't too nervous about this visit.

We waltzed through the foyer, which was thankfully empty, and up the stairs to her office. Same as yesterday, I knocked on her door and told to enter.

"Dean Wright," I said, approaching her desk. "You wanted to see me and my… friends?"

Her gaze flicked past me to the three massive men as we entered the room. "Yes. I wasn't aware that you were expecting company this holiday season."

I steeled myself, a nagging voice in the back of my mind insisting that since the dean was a Fae, she would see right through our ruse. Even so, I stuck to the plan, because I couldn't very well tell her they were demons who were here to do away with Sander La Croix.

She specifically ordered me to *not* go after that murderer. Was it still a *no-no* if I didn't lift a finger, and he was killed by demons instead? There was always a loop hole, right?

I casually utter my lie. "It was a last-minute thing. They wanted to surprise me by showing up unannounced. This is Drake, Arik, and Ty. They're snake shifters I met in Europe a few years ago."

Snake shifter–not demons–everything was just fine. Nothing to see here.

Dean Wright eyed them briefly before turning her full, penetrating attention on me. "I see." Her words seemed to have a double meaning. Or was I being paranoid? I'd never dreamed of lying to the dean before. Yet, that just happened. Could her Fae magic pick up on it?

She offered them a polite smile. "Welcome to Academy Obscura. I hope you have a pleasant stay with us. Miss Beaumont will surely be happy to show you around campus. We're the oldest college for supernaturals in America."

"We are most delighted to be here," Drake said. "Thank you for your hospitality."

Drake and the dean stared at each other for a long moment. Yeah, my snake demons didn't really look like regular snake shifters at all. Shifters appeared human when they were in their unshifted form. These guys? There was very little human about them.

Maybe snake shifters in Europe looked a bit different? Doubtful, but it was worth a shot. So far, it seemed to be working.

"My pleasure," said Dean Wright.

With an internal sigh of relief, I turned to go.

"Oh and, Charm?" she called out, keeping me behind while the demons strode into the hallway.

I faced her again, trying not to cringe. My pulse already betraying me with its wild flutter. "Yes?"

She pinned me with a pointed stare. "*He* arrives this afternoon. I wanted you to know. I think you two avoiding each other would be best."

My lips formed an *O*. "Thank you."

And just like that, my brain switched from being worried about Dean Wright calling me out on my bullshit lie, to raging over Sander La Croix setting foot anywhere near me. This academy was my safe place, my refuge, and that murderer was coming *here*.

Brow creased, I marched out the door. How could the authorities let that evil man go? That wasn't justice.

"Charm," Drake said. When I didn't respond, he tried again. "Charm?"

"What?" I snapped, stopping to face them in the corridor. Three pairs of snake's eyes were trained on me, questioning. I immediately felt guilty about being abrupt with them. They were supposedly here to help me, to do away with La Croix.

"I'm sorry." I ran a hand through my hair. "La Croix will be here in a couple of hours."

Drake nodded. "We shall wait for his arrival. In the meantime, perhaps you will show us around your world. It's most… peculiar."

"You really want to look around campus?" I guess it was a good distraction while we waited. Otherwise, I was going to drive myself insane, wrapped up in my dark thoughts and emotions. We couldn't do anything until that terrible man arrived.

Arik grunted an affirmative, and Drake said, "We do want to look around."

I glanced at the three of them. Ty leaned against the wall, looking bored.

"Okay, then. Follow me." I led them down to the Dean's Hall lobby, where the enormous, decorated tree stood with its glimmering lights. "It's winter and we're celebrating the season. Our main holiday is on the winter solstice, also known as Yule, which is the shortest day and longest night of the year," I explained.

They looked at the tree like it was the oddest sight they'd ever seen. I wasn't deterred, so I continued. "Traditionally we do fun things and eat sweets. Like these." I held out the plate of frosted cookies to them. Carefully, they each took one and, following my lead, took a bite.

Studying them as they experienced cookies for the first time, some of the tension drained from my shoulders. They certainly didn't appear very threatening right now.

Drake's and Arik's eyes lit up as the sugary sweetness exploded on their tastebuds.

Ty spit his bite onto the stone floor. "This is *disgusting.*"

I scowled at him, he was putting damper on our holiday cheer. "What are you, like the demon Grinch or something?"

He gave me a bewildered look and sneered. "What is a *Grinch?*"

"He's like a green furry dude who doesn't like— You know what? Never mind." I sighed, and finished my *delicious* cookie in one bite

"I'm neither green nor furry," Ty muttered, glaring at me.

I did my best to ignore the shiver that raced down my spine. Ty was one surly demon, did I really want to piss him off too much? He could snap me two, like a candy cane, with those enormous hands.

Speaking of which, candy canes and gingerbread went over about the same with the three demons. Arik ate an entire gingerbread house in the span of thirty seconds. He liked it that much.

Drake was more reserved, sucking on a single candy cane for the longest time. I could only imagine what his tongue was doing to that thing, and it made me envious. He seemed to know it, too, because he kept shooting me heated glances.

I finally had a breakthrough with Mr. Nothing-Is-Good-Enough-For-Me when I brought them down to the kitchen to see what Cook had stashed away for winter break. Ty was a goner at his first taste of brie. Though he'd never admit it, I knew I'd won as soon as he went back for a second serving of that cheese.

"It's good by itself, but it's even better on crackers or apple slices," I told him.

In response, he simply glared at me. But my nervousness around him eased a bit when he spread brie over a cracker and popped it into his mouth. He didn't spit it out. I called that success.

Then there was the spiced rum...

"You guys should probably slow down on that stuff," I said. "Remember that poison you sucked out of me last night? This is similar stuff. Don't drink too much."

Arik took another swig from the bottle and passed it to Ty. The horned demon took three solid gulps, probably just because I told them to slow down, before handing it to Drake.

What an ass.

I snatched the bottle from Drake, and capped it. "That's enough for now. Let's take this, the cheese and crackers, and those sweets back to my apartment. Come on."

They murmured their agreement. Gathering our loot, we made our way back to Academy Hall, which housed all the professors' apartments and offices.

As soon as I opened the door, the hairs on the back of my neck stood on end. I whipped my head around. Instantly, I spotted the cause.

Sander La Croix.

Our gazes collided, and the world fell away around

me. Rage and hatred barreled through my body. He'd murdered my parents. For that, I was going to make him pay. Evidence or not, I knew he'd done it. I'd seen him leaving my parents' house that night.

Okay, so it had been dark, and I'd only seen his silhouette, but I knew in my gut that it was him. I sensed him that night, and at the line-up, just as I had known he was here before I saw him.

He was guilty, even if I couldn't prove it.

Without realizing I'd reached for my wand. It was in my free hand, pointed at La Croix. He was dressed in a dark wool trench coat and tall black boots. His light brown hair fell artfully across his forehead, drawing attention to his amused hazel eyes. A faint smile appeared on his lips as he raised his hands in mock-surrender.

That wasn't going to save his skin. I wanted him on his knees, begging for his life, before I finally finished him.

I stepped forward, taking aim.

Before I could cast my spell, Drake hauled me into his arms.

I yelped.

Without a word, he picked me up, and carried me up the stairs.

"What are you doing?" I sputtered. "Put me down! I'm going to kill him!"

"Not yet." He held me in a vise-like grip until we entered my apartment. "We're predators, and we will strike when the time is right. Not before then."

The door slammed behind us. I huffed when he finally released me.

Waving the bottle of spiced rum in his face, I said, "I could have killed him right then and there! You could have too."

We missed a perfect opportunity. Whose side were these demons on, anyway?

Frustrated, I popped the top off, and took a swig of the booze. It burned all the way down my throat.

"We will, when the time is right, love. You have our promise." Drake tried to soothe me, but I was so damn angry.

My greatest enemy was within these walls. So close, I could feel him. My skin crawled.

CHARM

❄

Stuffed with sweets and cheese, and nicely buzzed from the spiced rum, we hung out in my apartment. My head was nestled in Drake's lap, with my legs draped across Arik's thighs. Ty sat on the fur rug in front of the fireplace, staring into the flames.

The apartment was heavily warded to protect us from La Croix. Not that I expected him to try to take on all four of us at once. He was a murderer, but he wasn't stupid.

Settled in with my demons, I sighed. I seemed to have two settings these days: horny or angry. At this particular moment, I was letting my wrath fall away in favor of sexual frustration.

Arik massaged my feet, and it felt so good that I let out a low moan. Though I could think of several other places I'd welcome his touch.

Drake gazed down at me, his slitted pupils mesmerizing. "I've missed that sound."

"Yeah?" I traced the markings on the back of his hand. Lying on his lap was like second nature to me, even though I'd never done it before in real life. Because of the dreams we shared, I was so accustomed to the way he felt, his voice, his touch. It was like we'd known each other for a long time.

All of that, and the booze, helped me relax in their presence. If they had nefarious intentions toward me, they would have acted on them already, right? They had plenty of chances to do whatever they wanted to me at this point.

So far, they'd been perfect gentlemen. Ty was grouchy, but he hadn't actually done anything threatening.

I cupped Drake's cheek. "Why did you come to me in my dreams?"

He leaned closer. "Do you remember those dreams, love? Do you recall what I said to you?"

I thought back to his whispers in the dark. Phrases popped to mind. *We will come for you, Charm. This is meant to be. You're mine.*

"Yes. I remember." I licked my lips, and his gaze followed the motion.

"Good." His blue eyes trapped mine for a long moment. "You're *mine*. Do you know what that means?"

I shook my head.

"You will." He closed the distance between us and

devoured me with a kiss. I parted my lips, and his forked tongue slid into my mouth. I shivered at the sensation, so foreign and yet familiar at the same time.

Heat scorched through my veins. Every nerve ending strained for more, and more.

Drake pulled away, then lifted me until I was straddling him. He took my jaw in one of his strong hands, but instead of kissing me again, he angled my head toward Arik.

I gazed at the quiet demon.

"Do you remember him?" Drake murmured. "Do you want to taste him, too?"

Arik's green gaze burned with desire. Of the three of them, he was the tallest and broadest, like a fiery-haired Viking with a snakeskin tattoo covering his body. He didn't speak much, but any guy who could rub a woman's feet like that was worth paying attention to. Plus, I did remember him, his touches, and his kisses. The deep rumble of his seldom-used voice.

I glanced at Drake, somewhat confused by his word choice. "I thought you said I was *yours.*"

"You are mine. But we are a den of vipers, and that means you belong to *all* of us." The deep purr of his voice made my toes curl. Then his words registered.

"All of you?" I caught sight of Ty, who was intently watching us. I might be up for a sharing kind of arrangement with Arik and Drake, but I wasn't sure about Mr. Surly over by the fire. He was the one who'd always watched but had never come near. Had never touched me nor spoken. What was his part in all of this?

"Now we'll share you for real," Arik's deep voice growled. He plucked me out of Drake's lap and settled me on his own. "Do you want us to share you now like we do in your dreamland, gorgeous?"

That was the most words I'd ever heard him speak, and I didn't know what to say. It wasn't every day a girl was given that proposition.

Drake chuckled, making no move to steal me back as he gazed at us.

Arik continued, "I could whisper sweet nothings to you all night, like Drake does. Except I'm not that kind of guy. Which you know."

"Do I? What kind of guy are you?" My breath hitched as I felt him growing hard between my legs. We were both fully clothed, but his heat seared through my jeans.

"I like to *take* what is mine." He caught my chin and kissed me deeply. He tasted like cloves, sweet and spicy. I melted against him. My palms explored his vast, rock-hard chest.

When he'd all but kissed me senseless, he said, "Hm. Not yet, I sense. Later. Now let's play one of those games you mentioned earlier, gorgeous."

"Huh?" My addled brain took a second to catch up. My body was ready to take things to the next level, and he wanted to play a *game* right now? "Um, okay."

Disappointment settled in my stomach. I was so turned on, I desperately wanted to come.

Drake caught my attention with his smirk. Realization dawned. I narrowed my eyes. Were they slowly torturing me on purpose? This was foreplay, wasn't it? Damned demons.

I put some distance between these addictive demons and me by sitting on the coffee table opposite them. Games. Right. Hot demon sex later.

I inwardly pouted.

They wanted to play a game… "Let's play Truth or Dare. It's super easy to learn. I'll start, and I choose to tell you the truth about something. So ask me a question."

Arik flashed Drake a sinful grin. "Which of us is the better kisser?"

Wow, okay. Arik definitely got the gist of this game right away. I was beginning to like the chattier side of him. But I could tell he was going to be trouble.

"Um… Shit. Honestly, you're both really good kissers. I can't choose between you."

They seemed satisfied with that answer. Which was the truth.

"Now the game goes to the next person in the circle, and they have to choose either Truth or Dare. That means you're up, Arik."

Without hesitation, he said, "Dare."

"Gutsy. Okay…" I thought about it for a while. What would be a good dare for a demon? Or for a guy in general? Got it!

"I dare you to let me put lipstick on you, and you

have to wear it for the rest of the night." There was no way he'd go for that.

Drake barked a laugh. Ty rolled his eyes.

Arik grunted an affirmative, and I beamed at him. I guess I underestimated this demon.

Getting up, I grabbed a red that would go great with his hair. Sure enough, he let me smear it over his lips without complaint. When he left it on as we continued the game, I admired his confidence.

"Your turn, Ty," I sang. "Truth or Dare?"

"I'm not playing this stupid game." He glowered at Arik, who grinned at him.

"So… there's a punishment if you skip your turn or don't play at all."

Ty turned his glare on me. "What's that?"

I wanted to go for the ultimate shock factor, so I said, "You have to remove an article of clothing each time."

His dark brows rose as he considered me. "Fine, whatever." Ty unzipped his hoodie and shrugged out of it. Damn, I hadn't thought he'd agree to do it. Ty didn't agree to anything very easily–or ever.

I tore my gaze away from his sculpted body. "Drake, you're up."

"Truth."

Surprisingly, Ty jumped in. "Have you ever been in love before?" he asked Drake.

"I thought you weren't playing?" I half-heartedly complained.

"Since I'm being *forced* to play, then I'll play." Ty's

dark gaze settled on Drake. "Well? Answer the question."

Drake glared daggers at him. The tension in the room swelled, growing thick and stifling. Arik remained silent. We all waited for Drake's answer.

Jaw clenched, he finally said, "Yes."

"Elaborate," Ty demanded.

Uh… I started to suspect we weren't playing a game any longer. This felt more like an interrogation.

I was beyond curious, even though this was obviously something Drake didn't want to talk about, and Ty was pushing him into it. To what end, I wasn't sure.

"Her name was Brina," he said. "I—we—thought she was the one for us, but it turned out not to be so." Pain lashed through Drake's blue eyes.

Silence hung heavy in the air between all of us.

"You don't have to say any more," I softly said.

Whatever Ty was up to, he was obviously upsetting Drake. This was cruel.

"Yes he does," Ty insisted.

I faced off with the dark demon. "No, he doesn't. Why are you doing this to–"

"She died." Drake's statement captured my attention. My chest pinched.

Ty leaned forward, victory in his eyes. "Tell Charm how she died. Tell her what happened. She deserves the truth."

"That's really not necessary." I needed to intervene, or this was going to get out of hand. More so than it already was.

Drake clenched his jaw. "No, you should know the truth. Brina died because I killed her."

My lips parted. I searched his haunted gaze for answers, coming up with none.

"What? How?" I warily asked him. My chest squeezed tight.

He raked a hand through his wavy hair. Pain creased his features. "I wasn't careful, and I bit her. My venom killed her."

"It wasn't his fault," Arik said in a low tone, shaking his head. "But it could happen again. It could happen to you."

My brow pinched. "I don't understand. You bit me and drew out the alcohol…"

"That was different. I was careful. But sometimes, in the heat of the moment, it's not so easy to be careful." Drake's gaze dropped to the floor. "I killed her."

My heart ached, feeling for him. What an awful experience to lose your loved one like that. The guilt he must feel about it every day would be crippling.

I knew because I felt guilty about losing my parents. Oftentimes, I thought about how if I had arrived earlier that day, maybe I could have saved them. Were their deaths in part my fault?

I was supposed to have been home for Yule last year, but I'd taken a spontaneous trip with a friend instead, only arriving home late that dreadful night. If I'd been there earlier… I'd either have saved them, or died with them. Instead, I was left all alone in this world with my guilt and need for revenge.

I reached out for Drake's hand, wanting to touch him and soothe away some of that guilt. Or at least let him know that he wasn't alone and that it wasn't his fault. Bad things can happen for no reason.

"Drake, listen to me—"

Ty moved so quickly that I yelped in surprise. He caught me from behind and hauled me to my feet by my hair. My scalp burned. His grip around my body was like a vice.

Arik and Drake shot to their feet, their shoulders rigid. They wore matching expressions of concern.

"Let her go," Drake said, his voice full of authority. All signs of sorrow and regret were gone.

Arik hissed when Ty didn't obey the command. The tension in the air grew thicker. Everyone was on edge, and I wasn't sure what to do. Fear jolted through me like a lightning strike.

My wand was in my jeans pocket. If I could just…

As I reached for it, Ty twisted his hand in my hair, and I instinctively gripped his wrist to ease the pain.

"You're hurting me!" I struggled against him. "Let me go!"

"Be still or it'll hurt even more," he snarled.

I whimpered. Why was he doing this?

Drake and Arik glared, they looked like they were going to tear into Ty any moment.

"Release her," Drake commanded.

Ty shook his head. "We won't survive another false mate. Last time nearly ruined us. So, let's see if Charm is any different from Brina. Shall we?" Without warning, Ty bit down on my shoulder.

I screamed. Searing hot pain rocketed through my body, spreading like wildfire. My shriek grew louder. My vision blurred, dark spots hovered at the edges. I screwed my eyes shut in an attempt to escape the agony that pulsed through me.

Suddenly, Ty released me. I fell forward into Arik's arms, unable to hold myself upright.

"Look at her," Ty spat. "She's weak. I'm telling you she's not the Charmer. Just another girl who would fall prey to our venom. She'll be dead soon enough, which is best for all of us. We don't have a true mate. It's all lies."

My apartment door opened, then slammed shut as Ty stormed out.

"I'm going to kill him." Drake cursed.

I felt like I was burning up. Every inch of my skin was too sensitive, too hot. The worst fever of my life.

"Can you suck out the venom?" I weakly asked.

Even with everything that's happened, I didn't want to die. Not yet. This wasn't my time to go. I couldn't die while La Croix still walked this earth.

Drake's sorrowful features swam into my line of vision. "No. The venom spreads too quickly. I'm sorry." He kneeled beside me, taking my hand in his. "I'm so, so sorry. There's nothing anyone can do."

Arik held me tighter against his chest where he sat on the sofa. His expression was as pained as Drake's.

It took a long while for his words to sink in fully.

They were telling the truth. I was going to die from snake demon venom. Ty had bitten me, knowing there was no antidote or any way to survive. He sealed my fate. Ruthlessly.

He did this to prove a point. That I was expendable. Why did he hate me so much?

I licked my dry lips. "How long will this take?"

"Not long." Drake gently kissed me. "I will kill him. And I'll kill La Croix too. I promise to avenge you, love."

Well, at least that was something. Maybe going now wasn't so bad after all.

Now I could join my parents in the afterlife.

Charm passed out in my arms, her small frame feather light. My gut clenched. Was she dead? I lifted her chest to my ear and listened. There, ever so faint, was her heartbeat. She didn't have long.

Sorrow, rage, and acceptance whirled like a snow storm in my gut. I was also confused. Charm had dreamed of us. She'd visited us across realms. I'd completely believed that she was the one. How couldn't she be? It didn't make any sense. She couldn't die.

Drake roared, his fist connecting with the wall. "I'm going to kill Ty."

"I want to kill him too, but..." I cleared my throat, hating the words stuck there. "Maybe he did us a favor. If he's right, and she dies, then we've spared ourselves yet another false mate. We'll be spared the pain Brina brought us."

His sharp gaze snapped to mine. "Are you saying you won't mourn for Charm?"

"No. That's not what I'm saying." I held her closer, devastated, unwilling to let her go. "I just mean that we got in too deep with Brina. Just like Ty, I can't do that to myself again. If Charm isn't the one, then I'll mourn her, but I haven't yet given her my heart. Not fully." I eyed Drake. "Have you given her yours?"

He harshly turned away, giving me all the answer I needed. Drake fell hard and fast for Charm, I saw it with my own eyes. There was no stopping him.

Ty distanced himself from her as soon as she appeared. Understandably so. We were all young and naïve when we met Brina, Ty gave her his heart too quickly, too unconditionally. He was devastated when she didn't survive the mate bite.

He's right. We couldn't do it again.

Charm's face grew paler, her lips almost white. As I stared down at her, I realized one thing… maybe I had given her my heart. Because the closer she drifted towards death, the more panic filled my chest.

I fucking hated that there was nothing we can do.

"Lay her on the bed," Drake commanded. "She should pass peacefully." His tone was too cold, too distant, like he'd already escaped from here.

I tightened my hold on Charms small body. "She's fine right here."

"You have to let her go. Eventually."

I nodded, once. "Eventually."

The door opened. Ty peered in the room, his gaze zeroed in on Charm. "Is she gone?"

Drake grabbed him around the neck and hauled him into the apartment. He slammed Ty's back against the wall.

"How dare you show your face," he hissed. "You've ruined us. I'll never forgive you for what you've done."

Ty didn't even bother to fight back. "We're already ruined. Brina destroyed us, only our fated one can bring us back together. And that's *not her.*"

"I hate you!" Drake slammed him against the wall again, and again. Violence radiated off him in waves. "When we return to the Underworld, I swear I'll flay you inch by inch."

"Go ahead. I don't care." Ty seemed completely defeated.

Charm groaned, capturing all of our attention.

I checked for her heartbeat again. Still thumping. Her chest barely rose and fell, but she was still breathing.

"She's still with us." Hope colored my tone. I murmured in her ear, "Stay with us, gorgeous. Be the one, Charm, and make everything all right. Please. I'm begging you."

CHARM

❄

"She's still hanging on. I don't know how it's possible, but she's still with us." Drake's voice floated to me where I lay on my bed. At least, I was pretty sure that's where they'd put me. A soft pillow cradled my head. Sweat drenched my clothes and felt sticky on my skin.

"Maybe she's the Charmer," said Arik. "Maybe the prophecy is true."

"I doubt it—" Ty started.

"Don't you open your fucking mouth!" Drake roared. "The only reason you're alive right now is because she is too. As soon as she passes, your life is over. Forfeit."

Hissing and a faint rattling sound filled the room.

Ugh, why was I still alive? Not that I *wanted* to be dead. Not really. It was just kind of a strange feeling when I expected one outcome, prepared for it, and the opposite happened.

Don't get me wrong, I was thrilled to be alive. Except for… Actually, the searing agony had mostly gone away now too. Strange. Had my body somehow fought off the poison?

I didn't have any answers. All I knew was this wasn't the afterlife. My heart beat steadily in my chest, as my senses awakened. I felt alive.

Trying to move, my limbs felt heavy, exhausted. I groaned.

A second later, the bed dipped on both sides as two large bodies hovered over me. Their presence pressed in on me, without seeing them, I sensed their worry, fear, and tenuous hope.

I peeked up at them through my lashes. "Hi," I croaked. "I'm alive."

My gaze swept the room. Yep, I was still in my apartment. Everything appeared normal, like I hadn't flirted with death… for however long it had been.

Movement at the foot of the bed caught my attention. Ty stood there, gazing at me with an odd expression. He seemed relieved. Which I'd attribute to self-preservation, except that he also looked at me with awe and… Was that fondness? No, surely, I had to be hallucinating.

Ty didn't like me. He hated my guts. He'd tried to kill me. *Well, that sure backfired, didn't it, dude?*

Apparently, I was tougher than anyone guessed. Or maybe just lucky.

"How long was I out?" I moved to sit up, and Arik, his lips a faded crimson from the lipstick, helped, treating me like something precious and fragile.

Drake answered my question. "You slept all through the night and part of the morning. I think. Strange things are happening outside today." He gazed out the bank of windows near the kitchen. The day was certainly darker than usual, and was that... snow?

I stood, with Arik's assistance, to get a better look. The campus grounds were coated in white. A blustery wind made it seem like the snow was falling in multiple directions at once. A blizzard had moved in overnight.

"Hm," I said aloud. "We don't normally get this kind of weather here." Was it magic instead of nature? I wouldn't put it past La Croix to create such a diversion, but to what end? I didn't know, but I was going to find out.

The lights flickered and went out. In the distance, I heard the unmistakable boom of a transformer exploding. When the backup generators didn't kick in, I let out a heavy sigh. Was it just me, or had the air cooled considerably? The fireplace crackled, and I moved closer to it for warmth.

"What is happening out there?" Drake asked. "It looks cold."

"It is." I shivered. "It's called a blizzard. I need to get to the Dean's Hall and round up supplies before it gets any worse. We could be stuck inside for days."

"We will come with you." Arik pressed closer to me.

I nodded. "Let me change out of these old clothes. I'll be right back."

Grabbing fresh jeans and a sweater, I locked myself in the bathroom. There was still a tiny bit of hot water in the pipes that I used to rinse the sweat from my skin. Then I dressed in clean clothes. All the while, coming to terms with the fact that I'd lived.

What did it mean? They mentioned something about a prophecy, a mate, but... none of that made sense to me. Witches didn't have fated mates. Whoever they were looking for, it wasn't me, which gave me all kinds of mixed emotions that I didn't have time to sort through right now.

Exiting the bathroom, I went in search of my warmest pair of socks. Three sets of eyes bored into my back. Two I considered my allies, one my enemy. Spinning around, I faced them. My mind made up.

"We'll go get supplies. But not you," I said to Ty. "I don't want you anywhere near me. In fact, why don't you find some other apartment to stay in? I don't want you around."

"You're not getting rid of me that easily." He glowered. A flicker of hurt showed in his eyes, but I wasn't buying it. Actions spoke louder than words, and he'd made his intentions toward me *very* clear. I wasn't stupid enough to risk my life a second time.

"You tried to kill me. What more do you want,

besides to finish the job?" I glared, and folded my arms.

Arik placed his huge body between us, offering his protection.

Drake hissed at Ty. "Do as she commands. Stay here."

"No. I had a point to prove. It needed to be done, and we all know that." Ty glanced at his comrades before his gaze settled on me. "Soon enough, you'll understand why I had to do it."

I scoffed. "Somehow I doubt that."

"Once Drake decides to tell you the full truth, then you can judge me," he snarled. "Until then, I'm not apologizing for shit."

Asshole.

I craned my neck to look up at Drake. "What is he talking about? What haven't you told me? Is this about the mates and prophecies thing? If so, I'm not your girl."

Drake and Arik exchanged a loaded glance. Both of them pressed their lips together, their refusal to speak clearly written in every line of their bodies. Fury rushed through my veins. I almost *died* and they're still keeping secrets. Maybe it was time for these snake demons to go back to Hell. They shouldn't be here anyway.

"You know what? You can all just leave me alone." I grabbed a coat and pulled it on, then stuffed my feet into a pair of rain boots. No, I didn't have snow boots, because it never freaking snowed around here. Folding my arms, I stomped out of my apartment.

Of course, they followed. I rolled my eyes.

The hallway was at least ten degrees chillier than my room. The farther I ventured, the cooler the temperature dropped. On the main level, the stone floor was frozen and slippery with ice. The demons continued to follow me right to the double doors.

"Charm, don't go." Drake grabbed my arm, pulling me against him. "La Croix could be out there. We—" He shook his head in frustration. "We can't go out there. We'd never survive the trek to the next hall."

"Because?"

Drake frowned.

Then it hit me. "You're cold-blooded. The sub-freezing temperature is too much for you, isn't it?"

Arik grunted. "Unfortunately, yes. Our bodies will shut down."

Some of my anger at them melted away. This was their weakness, and I was going to bet that someone on campus knew about my snake demons and had created this unnatural weather.

I licked my lips, considering my options. We needed food, or we'd never survive the storm. I was the only one who could go out there and make it back. So really, there were no options but one.

"I'll be careful. La Croix is devious, but he's nothing special." I tilted my head back to stare Drake in the eye. "I can take care of myself, you know. I'll be back soon. Go keep warm by the fire in my apartment." My gaze cut to Ty. "Even you. For now."

I wasn't so heartless that I'd wish Ty a slow, freezing death. Though he probably deserved it.

"Don't—" Drake started.

I broke free of his grip and bolted out the door. Nothing would be gained by standing around and arguing with them while the storm worsened. We could talk when I got back.

Outside, the wind bombarded me, whipping my hair into my face and tugging at my coat. I drew my wand and cast a protective bubble around myself. Even so, navigating through the thick snowfall was difficult. I believed I was heading in the right direction but couldn't be sure as there were no visible landmarks. The campus had turned into a shapeless, gray and white void.

I generally had a good sense of direction, but not when the world around me all looked the same. Swirling white grew thicker around my sphere as I ventured further into the storm.

After walking for ten minutes, far longer than was necessary to reach the Dean's Hall next door, I began to worry. At least the campus had a high wall all the way around it. I couldn't actually roam off into the surrounding forest.

However, at some point, I'd grow tired, and my magic would peter out. Then I'd be stuck out here alone. Potentially walking in circles until I finally collapsed.

Freezing to death didn't sound like much fun. So I pressed onward. Campus held plenty of buildings, so I was bound to run into one of them soon.

Another few steps and I swore I heard someone calling my name through the endless howl of the wind. Turning in a tight circle, I searched for the source.

There it was.

A dark figure emerged from the gloomy white. My heart stopped, and I froze, my mind racing with possible options for my next move. Because I wasn't going to let Sander La Croix kill me and bury my body in the snow.

CHARM

La Croix gestured with his wand. "Dean's Hall is that way. Come with me," he hollered over the brutal wind. I could barely hear him through our two protective bubble shields.

I gritted my teeth. It would be a cold day in hell when I let Sander La Croix *help* me. He'd sooner lure me into a trap then get me to safety. I was sure of it.

A tense moment passed between us as we stared at each other. The storm raged around us, as if egging us on.

Fight. Revenge. This is your chance.

I held steady, wanting him to reveal his intentions before I did.

A moment later, he cracked. A smirk twisted his lips.

La Croix pointed his wand at me, and I leveled mine on him, preparing for his attack. A powerful bolt of energy shot toward me. I widened my feet, bracing myself.

His magic all but shredded my protective bubble. I threw all of my energy into defensive magic—not my strong suit, but neither were offensive spells.

My gifts were in manipulating objects, which was usually quite helpful. Not right now, not during a life or death battle.

He bombarded me with magic. The force of it stole my breath.

In a matter of seconds, I realized that La Croix was a much stronger witch than I. More powerful. Seasoned. Ruthless.

Shit. I'd underestimated him, after all. *Stupid, stupid, Charm.*

His next round of spells obliterated my shield. I backed away, tossing whatever magic at him I could think of on the spot.

Think, Charm. Use your skills!

I glanced around at the whirling white, unable to locate a single object that could help me against my enemy. I couldn't see anything through this snow storm. Defeat knocked against my chest. But I refused to surrender to La Croix… I'd rather die.

Wait. In a way, this blizzard was an object. Inspired, I cast a spell to take control of the wind, directing it at La Croix until he was pelted with snow and gone from sight. Hopefully buried under ten feet of the powdery white stuff. Even so, I didn't let up until my hands started to shake from the effort.

Letting my magic peter out, I waited a minute, prepared to use the elements to blast him into oblivion. My pounding heartbeat drowned out all other sounds. My chest heaved with each labored breath.

I waited, rooted in place. Had I finally killed the evil man? Was that it?

When he didn't reappear, I figured that it was done. He was either dead or had given up and run away.

Then I heard it.

A second later, his laughter echoed through the blizzard. It surrounded me like an eerie blanket. I shuddered at the sound.

In the blink of an eye, La Croix stood right in front of me. Surprised, I had no time to react. He snatched my wand, then hauled me over his shoulder. I screamed, my cry lost in the wind. Then he sped across campus at a supernatural speed. Panic drenched me in a cold sweat.

I barely had time to catch my breath before we were inside the Dean's Hall lobby. My head whirled.

This was all *wrong*. Witches couldn't move that fast —we didn't move like *that*—even with magic to aid us. Only one type of supernatural could sprint that fast.

What was he? My gut twisted with dread. I didn't want to face the truth.

He dropped me to my feet and pinned me against the smooth stone wall, holding both of my wrists above my head. His wand pressed into the underside of my chin, forcing my head back. Glaring up at him, I noted the distinctive silver glow of his eyes and fangs protruding from his mouth. The reality of his nature slapped me in the face.

"You're a hybrid," I said in an accusing tone.

He smiled, giving me a full view of those deadly fangs. "Very good, little girl. I am. I'm half witch and half vampire."

I groaned, defeat settling like a stone in my stomach. Hybrids were powerful creatures. And now I was all alone with one who wanted to end me. Rage flared in my chest at the realization I might never avenge my parents' deaths. Heat burned behind my eyes, but I wasn't going to spill the angry tears that threatened to fall. I wouldn't give La Croix the satisfaction.

"Shh… Charm. I only want to talk to you." His tone was soothing, despite his wand pressed threateningly to my throat. "Do you know why I killed your parents?"

My whole body jerked at his admission. He was guilty, he even admitted it. After all this time of no one believing me, I felt vindicated, to a certain degree. Now that I knew the truth, it was only a matter of time before La Croix silenced me. Wasn't it?

"Why?" I rasped.

"Because they were neglecting their duty as guardians." He leaned down, close to my ear. "I know about the snake demons in your apartment. You're breaking your guardian family's oath by allowing them to be here. I can't allow that. When one bloodline fails to protect our realm from the creatures of the

Underworld, another bloodline must rise to take its place."

"I don't know what you're talking about." It was the truth. My family weren't guardians of any kind. We were normal witches, like everyone else, nothing too special among my type. I wasn't going to let this murderer make excuses—blaming *my family*—for his actions. "You're a *liar*."

He studied me for a long moment. The silence stretched between us.

"Oh, Charm, it seems they kept you in the dark. Or perhaps you're not yet at the Age of Initiation. When do you turn twenty-two?" he asked, peering into my eyes. When I didn't answer him, he said, "If I'm not mistaken, your birthday is in two days. You shouldn't even have *this* yet." La Croix fondled my charm bracelet.

"Get off of me," I said through gritted teeth. Obviously this creep had been stalking me, he knows my birth date. What else does he know?

He leans closer. "Think about what I said. You're the last in your family line of guardians, and if you don't take up the mantle, *I will*." In a flash of speed, he disappeared, leaving me shaking with rage all alone in the lobby.

My wand hovered before me, where he'd left it, and I angrily plucked it from the air.

What in the hell was he talking about? I touched my bracelet. As usual, it was warm and hummed with faint magic. Was it the key to something bigger? Or was La Croix fucking with my head, making me question my family? I mean, it had opened a portal to the Underworld, and I figured the snake charms and my snake demons were no coincidence. I needed answers.

I had a sense that welcoming mysterious creatures from the Underworld might be a bit dangerous. But when they offered to help me avenge my parents, how could I say no? Was I playing with fire? Possibly.

When I got back to my apartment, I was going to grill those three demons until they spilled the whole truth.

"It's been too long. I'm going after her." I gazed out the window at the wall of whirling white stuff. It was so damn cold here, so unlike what I was used to in the Underworld.

"Why?" Arik growled. "You don't even like her."

His accusation stung. Still, he had every right to make it, because all I'd shown any of them was how much I hated Charm.

Only it wasn't true.

I'd bitten her, marked her as my mate. Like it or not, she and I were bonded together for eternity. Which might explain this itching feeling that's relentlessly plagued me since she left the apartment. Since she ventured out into that storm—alone. We never should have let her go.

I rounded on my brethren. "She's in danger. I can sense it. I'm going."

Drake marched to the door, anchoring himself in front of it. "You'll die if you go out there. Then you'll be no help to her whatsoever."

"Stop arguing. You're wasting time." I glared at him. "Let me pass."

"I'm not going to let you hurt yourself." Drake narrowed his eyes.

"She needs me–"

"You won't make it two steps! We shouldn't have let her go, but it's too late for that now." He grunted in frustration. "You're bonded to her, Ty, if you die you know what that will do to her. She won't survive it."

Cursing, I turned away from him. Arik caught my eye, his gaze stoney, cold. Yeah, yeah, I know I fucked up and now they both hate my guts.

Where's the damn gratitude? I revealed Charm as our true mate. They should be happy, thrilled even. Instead, I get the cold shoulder from both of them. That, or threats.

Charm's tied to me and only me, since neither of them have claimed her yet, so it's my responsibility to keep her safe. I can't do that locked in here with that deadly weather outside.

I scratched at my arms, but the itch seemed to be beneath my skin. "If you don't let me out that door, I swear I'll jump out this window. So what will it be?"

"Let him go," Arik said. His gaze bored into me. "If you do this and it hurts her, I'll hunt down your demon soul, resurrect you, and kill you all over again. Understand?"

Fair enough. I'd do the same if our roles were reversed.

With a nod, I glanced expectantly at Drake. For a long moment, he didn't budge. Stubborn bastard.

"Fine." Stepping aside, he muttered under his breath. "We're going with you."

I didn't have time to argue any longer. With a grunt, I stepped out of the apartment, Drake and Arik on my heels, and made it down to the main floor.

Cold seeped beneath my skin with startling speed and efficiency. The closer I got to the front doors, the more I realized they were right. I wasn't going to survive long out there.

But for her, I had to try.

"It's fucking freezing," Arik grumbled.

Drake murmured his agreement. "It's colder than I expected. Ty, don't do this."

I sped up, quickly covering the distance to the doors.

"Stop!" His command only urged me on.

Before they could stop me, I slipped through the front door and emerged into a perilous world of white. My need to get to Charm outweighed any sense of my survival instinct.

CHARM

The return journey was easier. I made it from the Dean's Hall to Academy Hall without incident. I'd taken enough from the campus kitchen to restock my own food supply four times over. Those demons better not be picky eaters—except for Ty not liking most sweets.

As I returned, I wasn't in the mood. My interaction with La Croix hung heavily on my mind and heart, like a hefty ornament dangling from a too thin branch. I might snap.

Arik and Drake met me at the door, their expressions tight, and I knew something was wrong. A quick sweep of the room showed that Ty was missing. Maybe he'd taken my advice and moved out. *Good riddance.*

"Ty went out into the storm after you," Drake said, his eyes worried. "We couldn't stop him. He could have killed you last night, and for that I want to punish him, but not like this."

Wait, what?

"I thought you said you'd freeze to death out there."

Drake nodded.

Sudden panic squeezed my chest. I wasn't sure why I was having this reaction. Ty was an asshole. He deserved whatever happened to him out there. Except… I couldn't just leave him in that storm to die.

"We need to find Ty. How long has he been gone?" I dropped all my grocery bags on the floor and grabbed two scarves, a hat and gloves this time, because damn, it was cold out there even with a bubble shield.

"Too long," Arik said with a frown. "It's probably too late."

Like hell it was. I turned around and bolted, retracing my steps to the front doors. Visibility was still shit outside, and the day had grown darker. I cast another bubble around myself to deflect the worst of the wind and snow, and set off into the whirling blizzard.

I couldn't believe I was out here to rescue Ty. But it was because of me that his life was in danger—he'd followed me for some reason—and I wasn't enough of a bitch to leave him in this storm.

Had he attempted to kill me? Yes. But sometimes, at least, I did the right thing just because it was the right thing to do.

Furthermore, this burning need to find him and

for him to be all right was strange. Unexplainable at the moment. I'd worry about its meaning later.

My list of things to deal with later was beginning to pile up: La Croix, guardians, portals, why the demons were really here, Ty trying to poison me, and now my sudden determination to rescue his probably frozen ass.

Later. I'd deal with it all later.

I'd made it about halfway to the Dean's Hall when I stumbled over Ty's body. He hadn't gotten too far. Why had he come out here knowing that this weather would kill him? Was he really that desperate to follow me? Did he think I was going to betray them? Probably. Either that, or he was trying to prove, once again, that he didn't take orders from me.

Stubborn, difficult, infuriating demon.

Dropping to my knees, I included him in my sphere of protection. I rolled him over. His eyes were closed and his breathing shallow, but he was alive. Relief flooded my veins like hot cocoa.

I tried to lift him up. He was too heavy and stiff for me to carry. But this was one problem my talents could solve. I cast a levitation charm and guided us back into Academy Hall.

Drake and Arik were in the corridor, and they helped to haul him into the apartment, being cautious with his horns. Checking on him, their brows furrowed with concern. He wasn't out of the woods yet.

"He needs a source of warmth if he wants any

chance of surviving." Drake's gaze landed on me. "I will come clean with you about everything, I promise. But right now, I need you to take off your clothes and share your body heat with Ty."

I balked, staring back at him in disbelief. I might be a generally good person, but I wasn't a saint. "Can't you put him in front of the fire to warm him up?" Even as I spoke, another part of me screamed to go to Ty and do everything in my power to save him.

What the fuck is wrong with me?

Drake shook his head. "It's not enough. He needs the fire, blankets, and… you. He needs everything we have, otherwise…"

Arik had already stripped Ty down, wrapped him in the thick comforter, and placed him in front of the blazing hearth. Ty's face was pale, his lips blue. He wasn't even shivering to try to warm up.

I only hesitated a second longer before giving in to my instincts. "Fine."

Ty was going to owe me big time for this. I took off my clothes, keenly aware of Drake and Arik watching my every movement. Naked, I slipped under the covers with Ty.

My skin prickled with both goose bumps and awareness. "Holy fuck, he's like an ice cube."

Arik and Drake huddled near us, seeking the fire's warmth, as I entwined my legs with Ty's. It was like hugging a snowbank, but gradually he began to thaw. Hints of color returned to his ashy skin.

Surprisingly, being this close to him, inhaling his

sharp spicy scent, felt as natural as it did with Drake and Arik. We fit together like we were made for each other.

You're ours. Mate.

Did they mean what I was beginning to suspect they meant by those things? How? It was impossible.

I awoke sometime later with a scorching hot body at my back and a hard cock pressed against my ass. Glancing down, I found a black-and-gray patterned arm draped over my shoulder. *Ty.*

I froze, unsure of what to do, until my anger at him took the lead on my emotions—because I refused to let my heart and hormones cloud my judgement. Which they were trying to do, and almost succeeding. A very large part of me wanted to forgive everything he'd done, to cuddle closer to him, to give into this strange sensation that had my pulse skittering.

Instead, I slid out from under the blanket and quickly dressed in a flannel pajama set with little snowflakes all over them, then sat cross-legged on the sofa. "Start talking. I want answers. Right. Now."

Arik stood by the door, guarding us even though my protective ward was still in place. He watched me with his bright green eyes, but remained silent. A sentinel.

Ty stirred from his slumber and sat up, keeping the

comforter over his lap. Gazing at me, he opened his mouth to speak, but Drake cut him off.

"We were hoping that by granting your Yuletide wish, we could win your affection. Court you slowly, in this new realm, until you *chose* us." Drake grimaced. "But that's not how it happened. Now you're bonded to us. We've taken that choice away from you without meaning to do it."

"What—?" I wasn't entirely sure what he was talking about. Bonded?

Drake plowed on, as if he needed to get the words out as quickly as possible. "We've been searching for our true mate for a long, long time. We thought Brina was it for us. All the signs were there, but we were mistaken." He swallowed hard. "Her death nearly tore our den apart. Which is why Ty bit you. He would rather rush the mating process than see us get attached to another potential mate, only to have her die. We wouldn't survive such an outcome a second time."

I was quiet for a while, mulling over his words. Many questions that I needed to sort through stacked up in my mind. On top of that, I was trying not to panic.

Mate? Mating process? What had I gotten myself into?

Finally, I said, "Tell me about the mates thing."

Ty spoke up. "Do you not have fated mates in this world?"

"We do... but witches don't. Fated mates are

reserved for shifters and vampires." I cautiously eyed Ty. "Is this why I feel differently toward you? I know, logically, I should hate you for trying to kill me, but I can't seem to hold on to that feeling. It's fleeting. Instead, I keep feeling all warm and fuzzy, and it's seriously messing with my head."

Ty cringed. "I did what I had to do for my den. For that, I won't apologize. To answer your question... Yes, you feel pulled to me because of the bond that I forced on you with my bite."

I pursed my lips. This couldn't be happening. Out of all of them, I was bonded to this jerk? I couldn't even deal with that right now.

Then a thought occurred to me. "Is there a way to undo the bond?"

Arik shook his head. "No. There is not. It's a mate bond for life."

Heat boiled through me. I'd spoken too soon about my waning anger for Ty. Seething, I pointed at him. "How *dare* you? You took away my free will!"

"I did what I had to do. As I said before, I'm not sorry. Besides, we're demons. Not exactly the *good* guys." Ty's features twisted with a sneer. "What's done is done. We *both* have to live with it."

My eyes narrowed. "I hate you."

"I know. As you should." But he didn't say it back. Have his feelings toward me changed?

My glare deepened. As much as I hated to admit it, he was right. It was done. I was bonded to him and there was no going back. That didn't mean I had to like it. Dwelling on it, however, would get me nowhere.

While witches didn't have fated mates, apparently a demon's bite could change that in a second. Ugh. Was it my imagination, or was my life in a downward spiral?

Changing the subject, I said, "La Croix mentioned something about my family being guardians and how letting you three be here was basically betraying my ancestors. Do you have any idea what he's talking about?"

They exchanged several pointed glances. No one spoke for several long moments, and I finally lost my patience. "You told me you'd tell the truth! I need answers."

Drake nodded. "Very well. No, we're not supposed to be here. We belong in the Underworld. What La Croix told you is true. Your family has protected this world from ours for centuries. Otherwise, your world would be overrun with demons. Very few hold keys to open portals. Your family is one of them, and now that responsibility falls on your shoulders."

Holy shit. I was a guardian. And according to everyone, I royally messed up.

He continued, "However, our search for our mate led us to you. Now it is confirmed that you're our Snake Charmer, our fated one, and we will not be leaving here without you, love. You're *ours*."

My mouth suddenly went dry. The room felt too crowded, with their three massive bodies looming so close. All of them stared at me with hunger in their slitted eyes. They were predators, and once again, I felt like prey. There was no way out of this, I'd never escape them.

A tendril of fear unfurled and wrapped itself around my heart. What had I gotten myself into? I was certainly in over my head.

CHARM

Fated mate bond bullshit wasn't going to stop me from doing what was right. I owed it to my family to keep our oath and do the guardian thing—whatever that was. As much as it pained me, I needed to send these demons back to the Underworld.

I may have seriously fucked up, but I could make it all right. I had to.

To get some space from them, I dressed in warm clothing and took the winding stairs up to Academy Hall's turret. From here, I could see the blizzard beginning to calm and leave campus coated in pristine, fluffy snow. It looked like a winter wonderland out there. Normally, I would have enjoyed it, but with my inner turmoil, I simply stood and stared, frowning at the gorgeous sight. Today had been one of the strangest days of my life.

I had very little clue as to what my family's role was in all of this, but Mom had given me the bracelet to protect. The one that had somehow opened a portal to the Underworld. That was some serious magic, which I needed to take seriously.

Demons weren't supposed to walk this earth. I'd done a very bad thing when I let them enter my apartment. Granted, I was intoxicated, but I should have known better. I could be upsetting the balance of magic and nature by letting them remain here. My only option was to correct my mistake before it was too late.

My mind was made up. They were going home as soon as I figured out how in the hell I'd opened that portal in the first place.

La Croix probably knew how to do it. Not that I was going to ask him. He'd made it perfectly clear that he was after my position, and willing to kill me for it, like he had murdered my parents. The revelations from our little chat had changed nothing between us. I would get my vengeance, with or without the demons' help.

If only my parents were here, I could get this all straightened out and understand what was going on. How had they supposedly failed as guardians? How had La Croix found out about it? Was I really the bad guy and La Croix the hero?

Even though I was alone, I adamantly shook my head. La Croix was a murderer. If I started placing value and ethical judgments on this situation... No, I couldn't go down that path.

Twisting the bracelet around my wrist, I once again noticed all the snake charms. The demons and this bracelet were definitely connected. Fuck if I knew how or what any of it meant, though. What I really needed right now was a Fae to filter through my memories and tell me what incantation my drunk ass had muttered to open that portal.

Unfortunately, the only Fae on campus was Dean Wright, and I wasn't about to turn to her for help either. She'd probably kick me out, or worse, I could end up in Grimsmore Prison for letting demons run around our protected, heavily warded campus. What the fuck had I been thinking? This was a mistake.

"You're going to send us back, aren't you?" Drake's voice startled me. He leaned in the doorway, his expression solemn.

"How did you guess that?" I hugged my middle.

He shrugged. "It wasn't difficult." Coming farther into the room, he continued, "You should remember that we've spent nearly a year with you, Charm. It wasn't all physical pleasure either."

He was right. Between mind-blowing dream orgasms, we'd talked—a lot. At the time, I thought they were nothing more than murmurs in the dark. A fantasy land where I could be myself and admit to my greatest fears, my desires, my vulnerabilities. An escape from my loss and sorrow. I had no idea that I was actually talking to a real being, a demon, or three.

"I know you well, Charm." Drake slowly approached, his muscles bunched like a predator ready to strike. He was keeping himself under tight control. "Give us a chance to prove ourselves to you. Even Ty has his admirable qualities once you unearth them."

I shook my head. "I can't. What I've done is wrong. None of you should be here." It hurt my heart to admit it, but it was the truth. Fate was cruel to create us for each other when we belonged in separate realms.

I no more belonged in the Underworld than they did here. That place could never be my home.

"Are you so sure, or is that your fear talking?" He loomed over me, trailing his knuckles across my jaw. "The Charm I know is brave. She makes decisions for herself and doesn't let anyone else influence her mind."

"Exactly." I trembled beneath his familiar touch. "Ty took my choice away from me."

"Are you sure you hadn't already chosen us?" He bent to speak in my ear. "Don't lie to yourself. You chose us way before you opened that portal. We both know that's true. Now that we're *real* to you, in the same realm as you, you're afraid. Why?"

"I-I—" Was I afraid? Yes. Yes, I was. "Because I'm confused. Because everything is moving too fast. And because you're so much *more* in a physical form than you were in my dreams."

"You're so much more too, love. I want to explore every part of your body and soul, like we have done so many times before, yet never like this." Drake nipped at my bottom lip. "Do you want that, too?"

My knees were growing weak from his closeness. My fear of his demon nature, and our quickly spiraling situation, only heightened my desire. He'd called me out. He was right. I had chosen him—them—many months ago. When I thought they would never be real.

Now that he had materialized in my realm, I was overwhelmed by his presence. Most of all, I was afraid of losing myself in him for real, forever, just as I'd done in my dreams.

Firmly, I held onto the threads of my sanity. "But you even admitted that my family guarded this realm against demons. How can I be your fated one and protector of this world at the same time?"

"I don't understand it either." His breath mingled with mine. "All I know is that this can't be wrong if it feels so right. Tell me you feel it too."

"I do," I whispered against his lips. "I want this—you."

Guilt and passion battled for dominance in my gut. This was wrong. No, it was right. It was… fate.

As soon as I surrendered to my desires, to him, warmth spread through me and radiated outward. Deep down in my soul, I felt the rightness of my decision. We were connected in a way I may never understand, and demon or not, he had my heart.

"As you wish." His deep voice shattered the rest of my defenses.

He lifted me, and I wrapped my legs around his hips as he crushed his lips against mine. My back hit the stone wall, and I arched against him. Our tongues tangled, our breaths mixed, and my body came alive.

"I need you. Now." I unzipped his hoodie and caressed his impressive blue-green colored chest. My hands skimmed lower, down to that enticing V that disappeared into his waistband.

Drake caught my wrists in one of his giant hands. "Not so fast, love."

"Why?" I put enough space between us to peer into his blue eyes. "It's not like we haven't had sex before."

He let out an awkward laugh. "Yeah, about that… We have had sex in your *dreams*, and in the dreamland things can be a bit different than they are in reality."

"Oh?" Intrigued, I glanced down at his crotch, then lifted a brow in question. What was he hiding down there?

"Let me show you what you're getting yourself into. Then you can decide if it's really what you want." He released me and took a step back. I immediately missed his warmth.

I eyed him. Color me curious as all hell. He popped his jeans button, then lowered the zipper, and my breath hitched as his *thing* was freed. He palmed it, then gave me a pointed look.

Uh…

"What is *that*?" My cheeks heated.

Real smooth, Charm. Obviously, it was his demon dick.

But it was also patterned in blue and green. On the underside were chevron shaped ridges, and small protrusions studded the rest of its length, making it quite… rough, textured.

Drake frowned at my expression. "It's one of my dicks."

"I know, I know, that was a stupid quest— Wait, did you say *one* of your dicks?" I tore my gaze away from his cock to meet his eyes.

"I did." He released an awkward chuckle. "Snake demons have two penises, one for each testicle. Of course, only one is out at any given time."

I snapped my hanging jaw shut. Okay, I was not expecting that at all. That's even weirder than the textured nubs. *Two dicks?* Or maybe this was Yuletide come early.

"Um, okay, is there anything else I should know about?" I stared at him, wide eyed.

He caressed his erect cock from base to tip. "Are you sure you want this in you, love?"

I gazed at it again, mesmerized. It did look especially reptilian. I found myself wondering what all those bumps and ridges would feel like. I licked my lips and nodded.

Drake groaned. "Fuck, Charm, you're perfect. I knew you were the one."

I melted like a snowman on a warm day under his praise. He closed the distance between us, then we were on each other, unable to get close enough.

In no time, he had me stripped bare and pressed up

against the wall again. Our kisses were sloppy and frantic. I wrapped my legs around his hips, then paused. Was I really going to do this?

Yes. Definitely.

I angled myself to take in his huge, reptilian cock. The stretch burned, but the pleasure made it worth it.

Drake watched my face as he inched inside my soaking wet pussy. I was so turned on, wetness dripped down my thighs. I gasped, shivered, and moaned as he hit places I'd never known could be pleasure spots before.

Holy demon cock.

"Does it feel good?" he asked once he was fully seated in me.

"Yes," I said with a moan. "So good."

A satisfied smile curled his lips. "Good. Now hang on, love."

That was the only warning I got before he pulled out to the tip, then drove back into my cunt with a punishing thrust.

Holy shit.

He pistoned into me, and my eyes rolled back in my head. This was most certainly nothing like our dream sex. It was way the fuck better, more intense, and I was going to come any second.

Relentlessly, he fucked me against the stone wall and my greedy pussy took all of him. I whimpered and moaned, holding onto his broad shoulders like my life depended on it.

Almost without warning, my entire body tensed as

an orgasm ripped through me. Sharp and intense. Drake captured my cry with his mouth but didn't slow his ruthless pace. He rode me through my first orgasm and coaxed another one out of me a few moments later.

"Holy shit." I sighed against his shoulder, gradually coming back to earth.

His body jerked as he found his own release. Drake crushed me to his chest, holding me like a cherished prize. "Was that okay? I didn't break you, did I?"

A satiated laugh rumbled in my throat. "No. That was more than okay. Amazing."

"Good, because I have another dick for you. Ride me this time." He withdrew, and set my feet on the floor. Crouching down, he settled with his back to the wall and his second hard cock in hand. Where the hell had that come from? Maybe… it had been stored inverted just like a real snake's penis? Huh. Fascinating.

"Come here and feel it." He beckoned me forward.

I did as I was told, taking his length into my palm and stroking him. He felt just as strange and erotic as I'd imagined.

Without waiting for him to ask, I climbed into his lap and sank down on his dick. Then I rode him. From this angle everything was different. Amazing. I wanted to ignore everything else until the world was just the two of us.

We must have stayed up in that turret for hours,

coming over and over again until we were both exhausted and sated.

CHARM

❄

When we returned to my apartment, I was reminded that Drake came as a package deal with two other demons. One who I'd missed. In my dreams, I always had Arik and Drake together. Being with only Drake for the first time had felt wonderful, but also like something—or someone— was missing.

Arik arched a brow at us, and I dragged him down into a scorching hot kiss. He threaded his fingers through my disheveled hair as his forked tongue swirled around my normal one.

We kissed each other until we were breathless. Then I stepped away from him to take a quick shower. Alone, as Drake wanted to speak with his comrades.

I glanced at the demon who always watched in my dreams. Ty's gaze lingered on me until I shut the bathroom door. He was so difficult to read, giving away nothing with his stoic, guarded expression.

Yet he was the one who'd bound himself to me, who'd taken that risk knowing that this could be the outcome. A slim chance, he'd thought at the time, but still possible. Now we were stuck together. All of us.

After showering the remnants of sex from my body, I emerged from the bathroom with wet hair and dressed in jeans and a sweater. I felt refreshed, my skin buzzing with afterglow.

As soon as I sat on the sofa, Arik left his post by the door to dote on me. He made sure I was comfortable, brought me sweet snacks and hot cocoa, then drew my legs across his thighs so he could massage my feet. A girl could really get used to that kind of treatment.

Drake showered, then joined us. He lifted me enough to sit on the couch and position me on his lap. I felt dwarfed between them. Pure, guilt-riddled bliss.

While I hadn't completely changed my mind about sending them back to the Underworld, I was going to give myself more time to explore whatever this was between all of us. Being near them felt too right to be wrong. I had to sort through this, to get to the bottom of it.

My gaze lifted to Ty. He tensed where he stood in the shadows, watching us. I couldn't figure out what his deal was. He obviously didn't like me, and I would bet that he was just as freaked out about biting and binding me to him as I was about it. He played it off like it was nothing. I didn't believe that for a second. He'd screwed up.

Maybe I could take Drake and Arik as my own, and make Ty live with his rash decision. We could still be mates and hate each other, right?

Oh gosh, when had I started thinking of them as my mates? Witches didn't have fated ones. This was all impossible, yet real as the blizzard outside.

All of a sudden, the lights flickered back on, the electricity restored. Through the windows, a low winter sun broke free of the cloud cover to cast a glaring light that reflected off the snow.

"Looks like the storm's over," I said. Our bliss bubble seemed to burst with that news. I suppose we couldn't hide in my apartment forever.

Arik muttered a sound of relief as he squeezed my toes and shot me a grin.

Ty peered out the window. "Hey, La Croix just went into the forest."

"Let's continue our hunt." Drake stood, and the rest of us scrambled to our feet.

Right. Back to reality. "Be careful. He's a witch-vampire hybrid and powerful. Worse, he knows what you are, and he'll be prepared."

They murmured their acknowledgement, unfazed by the revelation. Perhaps hybrids weren't as rare in the Underworld… or they didn't exist at all. Who knew?

After wrapping the demons in thick layers, scarves,

and hats, I grabbed my own coat and followed them out the door.

"Don't worry about us," Drake murmured. "We won't underestimate him."

"What exactly are we doing? Are we going to kill La Croix right now?" My shorter legs moved quickly to keep up with their long strides.

Arik chuckled. "Not yet, gorgeous. We'll watch him, then we'll wait."

"Uh, okay." I was impatient to avenge my parents. The sooner they kept their promise to me, the sooner we could sort out everything else. Though, honestly, I wasn't in a huge hurry to figure out this mate thing.

At some point over the past few hours, my perspective of these demons had changed. I no longer felt like their prey. They didn't scare me anymore. If anything, I felt... safe, cherished, protected.

My rational thought and my emotions warred with each other. I should fear them, they weren't supposed to be here. At the same time, I'd never felt this peaceful sense of belonging before–until them.

I was so confused.

Gazing up at Drake, I asked, "What are we watching and waiting for exactly?"

"By watching him, we can learn his mannerisms and habits," Drake explained. "We must get to know our prey first. Then we determine the best way to lie in wait, then strike. It takes time. But in the end, we are one hundred percent lethal."

Their process was fascinating, methodical, and

ruthless. I just hoped we didn't have to spend too much time in La Croix's company. He creeped me out. He was also a danger to us all. What if he struck first? He could kill me and send my demons back to the Underworld.

We followed his footprints through the forest behind Academy Hall. They led to a small clearing, where they abruptly disappeared. Magic hummed in the air, and I was positive La Croix had cast a concealment charm.

"He's here somewhere," I whispered.

"We know." Drake's tongue flicked out to taste the air. "We can smell him."

We spread out, senses on high alert. My nerves tingled with anticipation.

A disembodied voice boomed through the trees. "I'm so disappointed in you, Charm Beaumont. I see you've fallen for the demon-filth's lies."

We circled the clearing but couldn't find the source of La Croix's voice. Yet he was here, somewhere, spying on us.

"Come out and face us!" I yelled at the coward, my wand held at the ready.

"I think not. Enjoy your last day on earth, Charm. You've betrayed us all. Tomorrow you come of age and the Beaumont bloodline will end. Let me give you an early birthday gift." Wicked laughter echoed through the clearing, then suddenly cut short.

Okay, that was eerie as fuck.

The ground beneath us rumbled, like an earthquake. We came back together, holding onto each other for stability, but it was no use.

With a deafening sound, the earth cracked, splintered, then split open to swallow us whole. My pulse surged with fear.

I shrieked as I fell. Darkness cocooned me as Arik used his body to protect mine. He spun us midair. I landed on top of him with an *oomph*. His muscular body cushioned my fall as he held me tight to his chest.

As quickly as it began, the rumbling stopped. We scrambled to our feet. Gazing up, we stared as the ground above reformed, locking us beneath the earth. Our world engulfed in silence.

What the fuck kind of magic was that?

I cast a couple of light orbs to illuminate the cavern. Drake and Ty were right next to us, gazing in either direction of the tunnel we'd apparently fallen into.

Was this a trap? A means to a slow death? Or simply a momentary obstacle, meant to distance us from La Croix?

I gazed closer at our surroundings, noting that they actually looked familiar. I'd been here before. Squinting, I searched my memory. Yes, of course.

"There are catacombs under the academy grounds," I said. Freshman year I'd been trapped down here for an entire day and night. It had started as a prank. One that went terribly wrong. "If we go this way, we should eventually come out somewhere on campus, or at least nearby."

Getting out of the catacombs seemed like the least of my worries right now. La Croix was going to come for my head tomorrow. Worse, guilt twisted in my gut. Had I really betrayed my parents, their memory? I didn't want to believe a word out of my enemy's mouth, but what he said niggled at me so much that I wasn't able to simply shrug them off.

Arik rubbed circles on my back. "Don't worry about La Croix. We won't let him hurt you. His threats are meaningless as long as we are near you."

With La Croix's show of advanced magic, I was beginning to have my doubts. "Just be careful. He's a very powerful hybrid, as you just witnessed."

A rare grin spread across Arik's face. "Don't worry."

"The air is fresher in this direction," Ty said, gesturing to our left. His curved horns almost scraped the ceiling. "We should go this way."

"Yeah, that's the way I pointed," I grumbled.

Ty silently stared back at me. I rolled my eyes.

Guided by my hovering lights, and their apparent ability to see in the dark, we walked through the winding, seemingly endless tunnels, choosing our direction at each intersection based on the snake demons' senses. Which I was glad they had, since I'd long ago gotten turned around. Memories of the time I spent down here, cold and alone, haunted my mind.

We rounded a corner, and I stumbled.

"Wait. Is that a door?" I halted in front of a wooden slab imbedded in the stone wall. I didn't remember seeing that before.

Arik gave it a push, and it swung open on creaking hinges to reveal a small, dank room. Thankfully, it was a dank smell I recognized. My chest expanded with hope.

"I think we're in the sub-basement of the Dean's Hall." I'd been down here on multiple occasions to search for rare artifacts in storage to use in charms class. No other place on campus smelled quite like this one. Musty books, rotting wood, and for some reason, a hint of cinnamon.

From here, finding the exit proved easy enough. We climbed several staircases until natural light finally surrounded us. I was right, we were in the Dean's Hall.

Relief washed over me as we stepped into the lobby. The cheery atmosphere stood in stark contrast to the tunnels beneath us. The scent of fresh, warm cookies floated to my nose and made my mouth water. Most of the faculty who remained on campus were chatting in the plush seating area beside the Yule tree. They turned in unison to face us with shocked expressions.

Dean Wright was the first to speak. "What in the world happened to you all?"

I stared back at her, unsure what she meant. Glancing down, I caught sight of the grime covering my clothes, and thick, sticky threads of cobwebs.

Ew. Gross.

CHARM

"I was just giving my guests a *very* thorough tour of the grounds, Dean Wright." Wow, could I make up a more stupid-sounding lie? Why was I lying to the dean, anyway?

Partly because she'd threatened to fire me if I stirred up trouble with the man who was sitting there looking super chummy with Professor Till. In the back of my mind, I kept hearing La Croix's voice, *"You've betrayed us all."*

So, until I could prove the legitimacy of that statement, one way or the other, I was playing it safe by keeping all of this under wraps—as much as possible. No one was throwing accusations at me, so I figured this game was between La Croix and me.

The bastard even looked amused right now. I guess he thought it was funny to make us walk around in the dark passageways beneath campus for hours. Or however long we'd been down there.

"Excuse us. We're just going to go wash up." I jerked my thumb toward the door.

The snake demons and I moved as a unit toward the exit. A frown pulled at Dean Wright's lips, and I could tell she knew I was up to no good. My pace quickened.

Seriously, though, I was just trying to sort all of this out, so when the time came, I had a valid reason for her to *not* send me packing. I needed this job. I loved it here.

Since becoming an orphan, Academy Obscura was my home. And teaching was what I wanted to do with my life. Both of those things could be snatched away from me in a second. I had to be careful.

Luckily, we made it out the door without any delays. Outside, the day had turned into late afternoon. Soon the warming winter sunlight would fade, and the temperature would plummet. For now, it was beautiful. A delightful sight after being trapped underground.

I was going to make La Croix pay for that, too. As well as murdering my parents.

"A tour of the grounds?" Ty scoffed. "You're a terrible liar. Everyone could see right through you."

"I didn't hear any of *you* coming up with a quick excuse for why we're covered in filth." I shot a glare at him.

"No response would have been better than that

ridiculous lie." Ty strode ahead of me, and I glowered at his back. I'd really had enough of his attitude.

Arik and Drake watched as I slowed and bent down to scoop up a huge handful of slushy snow. I molded it into a sphere, and threw it at Ty. The snowball flew through the air and hit my target square between the shoulders. I grinned in triumph.

Ty stopped mid-stride. Slowly, he turned around, and his narrowed eyes found mine. "You do not want to pick a fight with me, princess?"

Princess?

"Oh, I'm pretty sure I do, actually." I formed another snowball in my hands and threw it. This time catching him right in the face. He blinked, stunned.

Arik laughed. Drake glanced between us with a concerned look on his face, probably wondering if he should stop us before this turned violent.

I wasn't ready to back down. My third snowball got Ty in the junk. He grunted, then leaped into motion.

Game on.

I dove around a stand of trees to shield myself, quickly forming my next projectile, and waited. Sure enough, he stalked after me. I let loose, and the slushy powder smacked him in the side of the head. A giggle tore free from my throat.

I had way too much pent-up anger thrumming through me right now. A relatively harmless snowball fight was a good way to release some of it. Sure, it was cold, but it wasn't going to kill him. Worst case... I blushed, thinking of my naked body pressed against Ty's.

Apparently, Arik and Drake didn't want to be left out. A flurry of tightly packed white orbs bombarded Ty and me. Who the hell's side were they on? It seemed to be every person for themselves.

Then in a twist I didn't see coming, Ty grabbed me and ducked behind the wide tree trunks, shielding me with his body.

"Truce?" he asked.

"For a minute." Every cell in my body was aware of Ty's nearness. My skin hummed with the sensation.

Quickly, I turned and began to rebuild a snowball stash. As soon as I had a good number, Ty and I retaliated, flinging them at the two snake demons who were poorly hidden behind a couple of shrubs. Curses erupted from them, and I let out a laugh.

Ty smiled. A real smile that lit up his hazel eyes. For several heartbeats, all I could do was stare at him in amazement. He looked so different when he was happy and relaxed. Less… asshole-ish.

On a whim, I grabbed a small chunk of ice and shoved it down the front of his shirt. He howled as the cold melted against his warmed skin. The glare he gave me promised pain, but his eyes held a hint of amusement.

Oh shit.

I made an attempt to dart away but was too slow, and with serpentine speed, he tackled me to the ground. My breath hitched and my heart stuttered as his huge, lithe body covered mine. He pressed against me, as if to soak in my heat. His expression changed from teasing menace to something more serious.

"Thank you for saving my life," he whispered. Leaning in, he placed a chaste kiss on my lips.

My mouth opened to respond—or maybe in shock —but he was already on his feet and walking away. That was a *thanks-and-dash* if I ever experienced one.

CHARM

As the clock tower struck midnight, anxiety pulsed through me. Today was officially my twenty-second birthday—my Age of Initiation, whatever that meant—and La Croix had promised to come for me, so I was a bundle of nervous energy.

"Shh, gorgeous. You're safe with us." Arik snuggled close enough he could probably hear my panicked little heartbeat. He wore *his* birthday suit, while I was dressed in an oversized T-shirt and panties. Even so, his skin warmed mine.

On my other side, Drake spoke into my ear. "You are safe with us, love. I promise. Do you need a distraction? Something to help you relax?" His fingers skimmed over my stomach and hooked onto the waistband of my underwear, slowly sliding them down. It was an offer, a suggestion. One I was more than willing to accept. Anything to distract me from my impending doom.

I helped Drake get me out of my panties, and Arik, noticing what we were doing, helped to strip off my shirt. Then they descended on me with their mouths, tongues, and hands. Just like in my old dreams. They caressed, sucked, and teased me until I was a moaning pile of writhing want between them. My skin burned, my pulse fluttered.

Arik alternated between his fingers and his forked tongue to tease my nipples. I arched my back in a silent demand for more.

Drake chuckled and spread my thighs wide. His tongue flicked out to play with my clit. *Oh dear, gods.* His tongue was truly sinful.

When he pumped two fingers into my dripping pussy, I moaned, sinking my fingers into his silky hair. They devoured every inch of me. Stroking and sucking, until my body trembled and a heavy ache blossomed low in my stomach.

I came hard, rocking my hips to ride out the wave of ecstasy. My eyelids fluttered, and I caught those distinctive yellow eyes gazing back at me from the shadows. Ty. The knowledge that he was watching us, in real life, had me growing hot and desperate again. I needed more. Right now.

Arik kneeled on the bed and lifted me so that my back was to his chest. "Do you like it dirty, gorgeous?" he whispered in my ear.

I didn't know exactly what he meant until he used

my own slickness to lube my asshole. At first, I stiffened. He murmured, low and soothing, and I began to relax. I was open to trying new things with my demons.

I trembled against him in anticipation. When he pushed one finger inside my ass, I moaned and writhed against him. All those ridges and bumps on his cock were going to feel amazing.

"That's a good girl." He continued to prepare me for his dick by pressing in two more wet fingers. "Drake's going to take your pretty little cunt while I fuck this tight asshole. What do you think of that?"

Hell yes. "Please," I practically begged.

Both demons wickedly chuckled. Drake took my hips, lined himself up, and sank into my pussy. Inch by sinful inch. I gripped his shoulders to steady myself between him and Arik.

Holy hell, a demon sandwich. I was so here for it.

"How does that feel, gorgeous?" Arik spoke low in my ear. "Do you love his monster cock in you? Can you imagine what all of my ridges are going to do to your ass when I fuck you?"

Damn, I am going to come just from his filthy mouth. Who knew the sweet, quiet demon had the dirtiest mind and liked to chat in the bedroom? It's always the quiet ones...

I figured his questions were rhetorical, so I just moaned and pressed my butt against his hot length. Arik got the message. He thrust his reptilian demon dick in my hole, and I shuddered.

As soon as they were both fully seated in me, they stilled. I felt so, so full. It was intense. I swear I could feel every subtle texture of their cocks. Every ridge and nodule pressed against my nerve bundles as pleasure coursed through me. My skin felt too hot, too tight. I wasn't going to last long.

Then my gaze cut to the side and crashed with Ty's. He had his black and grey cock in hand, slowly stroking it from base to tip. Even more intriguing, his tip glinted with a piercing.

Holy fuck.

Drake and Arik demanded my attention as they started to move. Slowly at first, then building up speed when I begged for more.

They found their own in-sync rhythm and utterly ruined me over and over until all my anxious thoughts were gone and my body was a limp, endorphin-and-cum-filled mess between them.

Bliss. Pure fucking bliss. Happy birthday to me.

The rest of my birthday was spent in my apartment with my demons. We tossed together some flour, salt, and water to make dough for Yule tree ornaments, then baked them.

Boy, were these guys creative.

"What do you think of this, gorgeous?" Arik asked with a devilish gleam in his green eyes, holding up a three-dimensional, quite realistic-looking snake demon dick.

I choked out a laugh. "Um… I'm sure you'll find a very special place for that on the Yule tree. Dean Wright will love it." We're going to have to sneak that one onto the tree.

"What colors should I paint it?" he asked, studying his work of art.

"Green and red for the holidays?" I suggested, snickering.

Ty shook his head. "It's a bad representation. It's far too small."

"Well, I didn't have enough dough to make it the right size." Arik sighed, then popped open the green glitter.

I hid a smirk as he started decorating his monster cock ornament, then went to see what Drake was working on. He was decorating a two-dimensional ring that ended with hands holding a crowned heart.

"What is this?" I asked.

Without looking up, he said, "It's called a Claddagh ring. It represents love, loyalty, and friendship."

"It's pretty." I was in awe, his level of artistry truly stunning.

"Not as pretty as the one I plan to give it to." Drake glanced up, and I nearly melted under the intensity of his gaze. He broke the moment by placing a searing kiss on my lips, then went back to focusing on his ornament.

With warm cheeks and butterflies in my stomach, I

wandered over to a scowling Ty. I peeked at his ball of dough. "What's wrong?"

He held it up to the light. "It's all wrong. It's supposed to be a snowball, but I can't get it right."

"Well, snowballs are normally not that deep of a blue. Try the white paint with some clear glitter." I handed him the paint, and our fingers brushed. A zap of electricity shot straight through me, and I nearly dropped the bottle.

"Thanks," Ty said, quickly taking the paint from me. "I'll try that."

I stared at his profile for a few seconds as he seemed to ignore me. Had he not felt that? Or was he choosing to not acknowledge it?

Arik barked a laugh, drawing my attention. "That's a cheery little cock, right there." He held up his ornament for all to see. Green and red and white striped it like a candy cane, and on the tip was a glittery snowflake cum.

Nice touch.

Honestly, I didn't feel any different now that my birthday had passed. Whatever this Age of Initiation was all about, I called bullshit. All witches came into their magic as teenagers, everyone knew that, not in their twenties.

Besides, I already had my full magical abilities. This was nothing more than La Croix trying to get inside my head, just like his threat to end the Beaumont bloodline on my birthday. The guy had issues.

From that moment on, I decided to stop listening to him and his lies. There were no guardians. No secret line of witches who protected this world from the Underworld. It was all a lie to distract me from what he'd done.

He'd murdered my parents because he was a sick fuck, not because they'd done anything wrong.

I was restless that night as my thoughts kept circling through La Croix's bullshit, my need for vengeance, and my irritation at Ty for ignoring our mate connection, which *he* had created.

Instead of mulling over these things for the hundredth time, I scooted out of bed, leaving my two snake demons fast asleep, and tip-toed toward the couch… Which was empty.

Snapping my gaze up, I searched the studio apartment for Ty. The bathroom door was open, so he wasn't in there. I peered deeper into the shadowed corners.

A flicker of slitted gold eyes was all the warning I had before he was on me, his hand over my mouth to muffle my startled scream. He'd moved so fast that for a moment, I thought he was a vampire.

Ty spoke into my ear. "Come with me. We need to talk."

I nodded.

Quickly and quietly, he led us out of the apartment

and down the stairs to the main floor, where all the professors' offices were located.

"Open it," he demanded.

It took me a second to realize we were standing in front of my office. Which could only be opened with my magic or my hand on the doorknob. Besides my apartment, it was the safest place for me on campus.

I reached out and twisted the knob, listening to the series of bolts unlocking through the thick wood. The door swung open on silent, well-oiled hinges, and Ty shoved me inside before him.

He released me, standing with his back to the closed door, and flicked on a lamp. Dressed in only a long, thin nightgown, I wasn't exactly warm. But that was the least of my worries as I stood there, returning Ty's silent stare.

"What's going on?" I finally asked, shivering in the dim light.

Ty dragged a hand through his short black hair. "You're—" he started, then shook his head, teeth clenched. After a second, he tried again. "I'm not good with women, or emotions, or… lots of other things that come so easily to those two." He looked skyward, and I knew he meant Drake and Arik.

"Okay…" I frowned, wondering what he was getting at.

He sighed. "I'm not heartless. I know I approached this all wrong. Now I'm not sure… what to do."

Silence stretched between us as I waited for him to continue. He wasn't giving me much to go on. Was he regretting our bond and not sure how to tell me that? Or was he asking for something else?

Cautiously, I moved closer to him, unsure of what to say, so I reached for him. With viper-fast speed, he caught my hand. I gasped. The sparks ignited in an instant, buzzing over my skin.

"Ty—"

"I've wanted you from the first moment I saw you in our dreamland." He tightened his hold on my hand, almost painfully, while drawing me closer to him. "I've always admired your love and loyalty to your family. Your thirst for not just vengeance but *justice*. You're a terrible liar, and even that, I love about you, princess."

I gaped up at him. Someone had surely body-snatched Ty and replaced him with this intense, honest, sweet-talking demon. Right?

He continued, "I've just never been brave enough to approach you, like Drake or even Arik. It was easier to push you away and… I'm sorry. Pushing you away and treating you badly are the last things I ever want to do to you." His voice dropped to a whisper, "Can you forgive me? Can we start over?"

Mind blown. Poof.

Ty was sorry *and* asked for my forgiveness? Yes, I'd heard him right. Perhaps surprisingly, I needed barely any time to formulate an answer. I wanted him with every fiber of my being.

Stunned by his confession and my own response, all I could do was nod.

He exhaled a shuddering sigh. "Thank you. I know I don't deserve it, but thank you."

My heart flipflopped. "You didn't really want me to die the night you bit me, did you?"

His features twisted with pain and regret. "Of course not. My greatest hope was that you were the one for us. I wanted to be the first to mark you." He leaned down and raked his fangs slowly along my neck, causing a prickling sensation to rush down my spine. "I want forever with you."

My shivers from the cold morphed into trembles of desire. "I want you, too."

My words hung heavy between us. Ty continued to grip my hand, his breathing shallow and his body tense. Was he... shy? Tentatively, I reached up and touched one of his huge, curved horns. A deep moan escaped from between his lips, and he closed his eyes.

"Touch me like that again," he spoke softly.

Encouraged, I stroked the length of his horn, and he shuddered. Fascinating.

"Why are you the only one with horns?" I asked, giving his other horn some attention too.

"Because I'm a slightly different type of demon. A horned viper demon, to be exact." His breath stuttered when I pressed my body to his, continuing to gently touch his horns. "Charm. Show me what to do." Ty's eyes opened, and they were molten gold.

My lips parted. "Show you... what to do?"

He nodded. "I've never..."

"Never what?" I frowned in confusion. He glanced

away, and I could swear a blush crept into his tanned cheeks. Silence stretched between us. Then it dawned on me. But it surely couldn't be possible. Could it?

"You're a virgin?" I tried to keep the disbelief out of my voice and failed.

He nodded again.

"But—but you guys had found Brina and thought she was your mate. Didn't you, you know, with her?" I waved one hand to indicate my meaning.

"I didn't, no." Ty released my hand and shuffled to the side, gaze downcast. "Never mind. This was a bad idea—"

I approached him as if he were the prey, instead of the other way around, for once—or at least a skittish, hesitant virgin snake demon. Impossible. But apparently not. Demon and virgin were two things that just didn't go together in my mind. They were like fruitcake with pepper jack cheese. Just no.

"Ty, it's okay. I was surprised, that's all. I'm sorry. Can we start again?" I asked, stepping into his space. Rising to my toes, palms flat against his chest, I kissed him. He hesitated a moment, then kissed me back with enthusiasm. My pulse sped up.

Encouraged, I slipped out of my nightgown and let it pool on the floor. Pulling back, Ty raked his gaze down my body in the dim light.

Tentatively, he touched my skin and his brows rose. "You're so soft."

I smiled up at him. "Touch me wherever you want."

He took me at my word, exploring my body with

both hands, and tasting my skin with flicks of his forked tongue. Growing bolder, he leaned down and nipped at my nipples with his fangs.

I gasped, and my flesh pebbled. I arched into him. He scraped his deadly, venomous canines over my skin, then watched its natural reaction with fascination.

"Ty," I moaned, panting. "I want you."

He let me guide him to sit on my desk and helped me undress him. As I uncovered every inch of black and grey patterned skin, anticipation sizzled through me. He had a pierced dick.

I climbed up to straddle his thighs, marveling at his unique cock. I stroked him, and his head fell back, so I kissed along the column of his neck. He groaned, the sound music to my ears.

Gently, letting him take in every moment of it, I lowered myself onto his hot, ridged length. He stretched me in the most delicious way. His texture pleasured me in all the right places, but somehow that piercing added even more to the experience.

Once I'd taken him all the way in, I undulated my hips, rocking against him. I swallowed my moan, not wanting to alarm him. He felt so damn good.

He muttered a curse.

"Is this okay?" I asked, reaching up to grip his horns. I didn't know how sensitive they were to pressure.

He bucked beneath me. "Fuck! Yes, hold on to my horns. Just like that."

He groaned, his strong hands finding my ass cheeks. I was glad I had something to hold on to because Ty quickly overcame his uncertainty and shyness. Gripping my thighs, he surged into my fluttering pussy. Over and over, until I cried out.

Ty glanced at my face, searching for any sign of pain and found none. I met each one of his thrusts, my tits bounding. He marveled at the sight.

Taking full control, he thoroughly fucked me, that piercing kept hitting me just right inside. Holding me in place, he squeezed every last drop of pleasure from my body.

He came the first time, with a groan and curse. I followed him over the edge, already on my third orgasm. Then he bent me over the desk and pounded into me from behind. This office, and especially my desk, was never going to be the same after tonight.

We fell to pieces together one last time, then slumped onto the thick wool area rug. Ty caught me up in a tight embrace. He kissed my hair, his breathing coming in short, rapid pants, just like mine.

"Thank you, princess. That was—wow."

I chuckled at his earnest tone. "Wow, indeed." I placed a kiss on his lips. "Though I'm not sure why you keep calling me *princess*. I just let you fuck me all over my office. There was nothing regal about any of what we just did."

He grinned down at me. I loved that smile that lit up his hazel eyes and softened his features. "No, but it was perfect." He sobered. "I call you princess because that is what you are to me, to us all, actually."

"I don't understand," I admitted.

"Drake, Arik, and I are princes in the Underworld. Now that we've claimed you, that makes you a princess. Our princess."

My mouth formed an *O*. Oh, shit. "Really? Why didn't any of you tell me before now?"

He shrugged. "It's not really that important. There are lots of princes of Hell, though only one king. You're what's important. Now that we've found you, princess, we're never letting you go. *I'm* never letting you go."

I gazed into his deep, golden eyes and believed every word.

CHARM

"The dean wants to see me… again," I told my demons over breakfast, waving the messenger parchment in the air. "Apparently, I need to pick up a package. Who wants to come with me? I don't know what La Croix is up to, but I don't trust that he's done with his evil games."

"Me," they all said in unison.

I grinned. "I don't think this calls for a group outing. It's a real quick there-and-back-again."

"I'll escort you, princess." Ty rose from his seat.

"I'm a better bodyguard," said Arik, also standing.

Drake leaned toward me. "You're going to have to choose."

Choose? I hated choosing between them for anything. But we'd drawn enough attention to ourselves already. Ty and I had just spent an amazing night together in my office, so I needed to spread around the love and attention.

"Arik, walk with me." There, decision made.

Arik puffed out his chest, and shot a smug grin at Ty. I sighed. But I knew full well that Ty would have gloated if I'd chosen him. So in the end, it was all fair.

Arik and I strolled across campus. The snow had mostly melted into puddles, except for the patches of it that remained on the shaded areas and in the trees. We walked close to each other, our arms brushing with each step.

"When do you think the time will be right to deal with La Croix?" I asked him.

"Soon, gorgeous." He grinned down at me.

"I've told you how powerful he is, and that he's half vampire. Yet, you all seem so confident that you can take him on. Why?" I was beyond curious. There was still so much I didn't know about my demon mates, I could sense it.

His smile widened. "Because we're snake demons."

Like that answered everything. I sighed.

"And… you have some kind of special power?" I wasn't aware of all of their abilities, but taking on a witch-vampire hybrid would be a huge task for anyone. Even a very powerful person.

"You have dragons in this realm, yes?" he asked.

I nodded.

"Like dragons, we are impervious to most witches' magic, especially when we're shifted. And a vampire's fangs cannot penetrate our skin. Don't worry so much, gorgeous." He looped his arm around my shoulders, holding me against his body while I pondered this new information.

That did, in fact, give them an advantage where La Croix was concerned. Maybe they really could defeat him.

We arrived at the Dean's Hall, but instead of going upstairs to the dean's office, the note had instructed me to pick up something in one of the sub-basement rooms. Probably another artifact to use for charms class next year. The new term started in a couple of weeks.

Or, this could be a trap.

"We should be careful," I insisted. "Just in case."

"I'll take the lead. Stay behind me." Arik gently positioned me behind his massive frame. I was grateful for his protection.

I descended the stairs behind him with my wand in hand and held at the ready. One could never be too careful with the likes of Sander La Croix lurking around.

The staircase spiraled around in a tight circle as it took us deep into the earth beneath the academy. We finally arrived in a long, damp corridor lit by magical, flaming torches. As soon as my feet hit the stone floor, my skin prickled with unease.

I reached out to Arik to stop him, just as a blast of icy magic shot toward him and encased him in a cube of ice. Horror zipped through my chest.

"No!" I spun, finding the caster.

Sure enough, La Croix approached, a triumphant smirk on his lips. Arik had said that they were impervious to a witch's magic, but there were ways around that. Freezing him in an ice cube was honestly brilliant. But it also meant that La Croix knew what he was up against.

"Charm, dearest girl, hand over your bracelet, and I'll let you live," he said, keeping his wand trained on me.

I took a moment to pretend to think about it, rage leeching through my veins. "Mm… no. I'm done with your lies and threats."

"Are you?" An evil glint shone in his cruel eyes. "Then I'll just have to take it from you by force." He shot a wicked curse at me, which I miraculously managed to block.

"Why do you want my family's legacy so badly?" I asked, trying to distract him. I needed to thaw Arik before he died in there. As subtly as possible, I threw a fireball toward the block of ice, and it began to melt.

La Croix retaliated by bombarding me with magic and driving me farther along the hallway. One of his spells made contact with my arm. It burned right through the sweater and jacket, and seared my skin. I screamed.

Ducking into one of the rooms, I took cover beneath an old desk with a bunch of lamps and boxes piled on and around it. Pain seared my arm. My face flushed with exertion.

"Charm, you can't hide forever," La Croix taunted,

then a shelf of knickknacks exploded to my right. "You want to know the real reason I killed your parents?"

I did. But I wasn't going to verbalize my response and give away my location. For a fleeting moment, I was safe. But damn did this wound *hurt*.

It didn't matter, though, because La Croix seemed to love to hear himself talk. "That Yuletide night, I was looking for your charm bracelet. As you know, your mother always wore it, so I was there to take it off of her corpse. Imagine my surprise when it wasn't on her wrist any longer. All that time planning, gone to waste."

Another jarring crash sounded, this time farther to my right as a pile of wooden crates exploded. "It took me a while to figure out that she'd passed it on to you."

His next bolt of magic hit the desk I was under, and I gave a squeal as I darted away from the flying debris.

I rose and faced him, and we exchanged a volley of spells. Mine were no match for his ruthlessness.

La Croix sneered. "I don't think you know any dark magic spells, do you? Really, destroying you is going to be too easy. Then I'll tear that bracelet from your cooling corpse and summon my horde of demons from the Underworld."

My jaw dropped in disbelief. Incredulous, I shouted, "You! You don't want to be a guardian! You want to do the opposite. You fucking *liar*."

"Oh, come on. You didn't really think I was some noble prick trying to save this world, did you?" He laughed at my murderous expression. "I guess the thought had crossed your mind. Maybe you are too sweet of a girl, Charm, even able to see the very best in me."

He paused for a moment in thought, surveying me with a keen eye. "We could rule this world together… Imagine an army of demons at our beck and call. It's in your blood to walk between both realms. I think… I think we'd make an excellent team. What do you say?"

I scoffed. "Are you fucking kidding me?"

"I'm dead serious." He flashed his fangs. "Join me. Give me the bracelet. Or die. Those are your options."

A new wave of rage rushed over my skin, this time carrying a sense of power with it that I hadn't felt before. If La Croix was right and being a guardian was in my blood, then I had been chosen for this job. It was my destiny to protect this realm from people like him.

And from demons, a voice whispered in my mind. I shoved away that thought.

Magic crackled over and around me. My charm bracelet grew warmer and shone with a golden light. The power pulsing through me was heady, addictive. And in that moment, I knew that I was indeed a Guardian. As my parents had been before me, and it was a very important job.

The sudden *knowing* made me stagger and sway. Purpose filled me up, pulsating through my blood.

"You can try to take this bracelet from me, La Croix." I attacked him. Long-forgotten spells that I'd learned from my mother as a child spilled from my lips. Like an old nursery rhyme I hadn't heard in years, but never truly forgotten.

La Croix seemed to notice the change in me too, as he began to use not only magic but his vampiric speed to avoid getting hit by my spells.

In a matter of seconds, the room was completely destroyed as he and I went at each other with ruthless abandon. Small fires caught on fallen papers, wooden furniture lay in splinters, and the very air pulsed with static electricity.

I held my own against La Croix. A sudden viciousness took over, and I fought harder, until I had him backed into a corner.

He licked his lips, his gaze darting from side to side to find a way out. "I guess I underestimated you, girl."

"Now we've both made that mistake. Underestimated the other." With a zap of magic, I disarmed him, then summoned his wand to me. If he'd been a normal witch, that would have rendered him helpless, but he was also half vampire—deadly even without the use of magic.

"Do you have it in you to kill me, Charm?" He sank to his knees, and I knew it was a trick to make me lower my guard. So I kept my wand on him, ever alert. "Do it quickly. Avenge your parents. Do it now."

"*Don't* tell me what to do." I kept him there, debating about how to kill him. He was too cruel for a quick death. He'd certainly made my parents suffer before he finished them off. No, I wanted him to suffer too. Something slow and painful would be ideal.

Movement near the door caught my eye. That split second of a distraction was enough for La Croix to take the opportunity and lunge right at me. His body was about to collide with mine when an enormous snake swept him up into its hold.

I scrambled backwards until my spine hit the wall. Standing there, I stared at the three giant snakes, which crowded into the room.

Oh my gods!

Each was a different color, but that was all that told them apart. Well, and Ty's enormous, curved horns. A wave of relief washed over me as I recognized that the red-orange one was Arik and he was alive. Drake had been the one to snatch up La Croix, his blue and green scales gleaming in the flickering torch light.

La Croix screamed and cursed. He tried to sink his vampire fangs into Drake's flesh but never managed it.

Ty, his black and gray nearly blending with the shadows, hissed and snapped at La Croix. Drake held him firmly in his scaled coils. Then Ty and Arik repeatedly struck the witch-vampire hybrid. He cried out in pain, and my lips slowly spread into a smile. Their venom was the exact type of death I wanted for that bastard but couldn't deliver myself.

La Croix screamed and begged, writhed and whimpered. Blood dripped from his growing number of puncture wounds. His mouth frothed with poison.

I watched him die, thinking of the gruesome scene I'd come across when I'd entered my parents' house that Yuletide night. Blood sprayed the walls and soaked into the rugs, my mother's and father's muti-lated bodies splayed in unnatural positions. Unfortunately, I'd never be able to erase that memory. Every detail was seared into my brain.

Sander La Croix deserved what he was getting. And in honor of my parents, of their memory, I watched until his body went limp, his dead eyes staring into the void.

Drake uncoiled and dropped him onto the stone floor like a discarded rag doll.

The three snake demons slithered and coiled around each other in the tight space until they finally stepped from the shadows in their two-legged, human-ish forms.

Drake, Ty, and Arik rushed toward me, their hands searching my body for injuries.

"I'm okay," I insisted. A few scrapes, nicks, and burns, but nothing that a good healer couldn't fix. "He's dead." I voiced the obvious, because somehow saying it out loud made it more real.

He was dead, and this was over.

A flurry of emotions struck me all at once: relief, finality, peace, and… a sense of duty.

I untangled myself from the demons and stepped a few paces away, holding my wand pointed at them. "La Croix was right about one thing, though. My family are Guardians. I'm duty-bound to send you back to the Underworld. I'm sorry."

CHARM

❄

"I'm so sorry," I said again.

They just stood there, staring at me with blank expressions, which I realized was acceptance. They knew I spoke the truth.

"I'm a Guardian, a protector of this realm, and you're demons. We… can't be together." Heat pooled behind my eyes, and I blinked the tears away. I had to do this. There was no other choice without me being a complete hypocrite. I couldn't be with them and protect this world against them at the same time.

Us being together was… impossible. A fantasy. A dream.

With the Latin words I'd learned long ago on the tip of my tongue, I adjusted my grip on my wand and drew in a deep breath. I closed my eyes as I began to murmur the spell that would open a portal to the Underworld. I knew they wouldn't try to stop me.

My heart squeezed painfully in my chest. Suddenly, my words faltered, and I opened my eyes. Three pairs of familiar, sorrowful eyes gazed back at me and I… just couldn't. I couldn't go through with it.

I *loved* them.

The realization hit me like a speeding sled. I loved all three of them. A sob wrenched free from my throat as I fell to my knees.

Drake caught me up in his arms. "It's okay, love. Let's get you home."

I buried my face in his shoulder, crying, as he carried me back to my apartment. Why did being with him feel so right if it was supposed to be so wrong? This wasn't fair.

Over the next two days, I healed and struggled with my conscience. Dean Wright learned what had happened to Sander La Croix—the truth—and surprisingly took my side. Not only did she forgo calling in the authorities, but she kept me on at the academy. The official story she'd come up with was that La Croix had vanished in the blizzard and was presumed dead. That was good enough for me.

Yule morning rolled around. I woke up next to a warm body, Arik, and felt a pang of guilt as I reached out for him. While my mind told me it was wrong, my heart and intuition said the opposite. I was torn, spending every moment in a holding pattern.

We couldn't go on forever like this, I knew that, but I needed a little more time. Just to the new year. At least, that's what I kept promising myself.

Arik rolled toward me with a sleepy smile. "Morning, gorgeous."

Like a wanton vixen, I pushed him down, then climbed on top of my big Viking demon and straddled his hips. He was already hard. I was wet and ready.

I kissed him softly as I eased down on his ridged cock, taking him into my body. He groaned as we began to move together. A rhythm that had begun to be familiar, comfortable, desirable.

I knew without looking that we were alone in my apartment. Briefly, I wondered where Drake and Ty had gone off to. Wherever it was, they'd be back soon.

I rode Arik harder, chasing my first orgasm. His hips pumped up to meet mine as he teased my nipples, one breast in each of his large hands. I was right on the verge of falling over the precipice when the door crashed open and slammed into the wall.

"What the fuck?" Arik snarled, as I yelped in surprise.

Drake and Ty rushed through the door, slamming it closed behind them. I climbed off Arik with a glare. I'd been so close to coming.

"What are you guys doing?" I demanded, pulling a sheet around me.

Ty dropped a heavy tome on the foot of the bed and opened it to a specific page. "Read this."

I scowled up at him, but ultimately, curiosity won out over the frustration of my interrupted orgasm. I peered at the page, then glanced at the cover. It was an old Beaumont family grimoire. Father had given me most of the library when I'd secured my teacher's assistant job here. He knew how it was my dream, and unless I was fired, I'd eventually become a full-time professor at Academy Obscura. I'd received the good news of my acceptance during my senior year.

While I'd had this huge collection of old family grimoires, I'd had yet to go through them with the death of my parents, then graduation, my new teaching position, then the stress of La Croix's numerous court appearances.

I'd spent the past year so focused on his case, on avenging my parents, that every ounce of energy I could spare, I poured into making sure he got convicted. Then the justice system failed me.

The grimoires were still packed in boxes stacked in a corner of my office. Honestly, they'd kind of slipped my mind. With everything else going on, they seemed unimportant. Until now, perhaps.

I read over the page, wondering what I was looking for specifically. This tome was an especially old one, dating back several hundred years, and written by a great-great-somebody Beaumont.

One passage caught my eye.

Every eighth generation, a Charmer, a special type of Guardian, is born and fated to the snake demon princes of the Underworld to protect both realms.

Wait, what the *what*? I read the passage again. And again.

It went on to explain how usually Guardians lived out normal lives here on Earth, but a Charmer could navigate between realms as she wished and often lived a more unique, and much longer life.

My heartbeat stuttered. That meant…

I eventually dragged my gaze away from the page to stare at Ty and Drake.

Arik snatched up the grimoire and read it for himself. "Oh, shit. Wow."

Ty kneeled in front of me, taking my face between his hands. "We're your demon princes, and you are our snake Charmer, princess. We are meant to be together. Don't you see? It's all in that book."

I did see. Finally, I saw that my heart had been right all along. We were fated, destined for each other and an adventurous life together. Hope blossomed in my chest.

I leaned forward and captured his lips with mine. I poured all my understanding into that kiss, then wrapped my arms around him and dragged him into bed. Arik looped an arm around my waist, and he stole a kiss before giving me back to Ty.

Drake strode forward. "Does this mean you will make us yours, love?"

"Yes." I beamed. This was the best Yuletide gift ever. "Yes. Now come to bed. I want to celebrate Yule in the best way I can think of right now."

"As you wish." He stripped, then climbed in with us.

The mattress dipped under all of our combined weight. Their nearness felt like an electrical current sparking across my skin, sensitizing every inch of my body.

Arik drew me closer to finish what we'd started. I sank down on him with a low moan.

From behind me, Drake wound my hair around his fist and angled my head to the side. Anticipation prickled across my skin.

"Now you're ours, love." He eased into me from behind, filing me up. Then his fangs pierced the delicate skin at my neck.

Arik sat up enough to mark one of my breasts with his own bite. I moaned, surrendering to their claiming. The bond slithered through my body and coiled around my heart.

I was theirs.

Forever.

Seeming satisfied with their claim on my heart and soul, they focused on pleasuring my body. Their unique cocks stroked places in me that I hadn't realized could feel so good before being with them.

I glanced at Ty, who'd undressed. As if my attention were an invitation, he came closer and stood, his ridged, pierced cock bobbed in my face. I opened my mouth and took him in. His dick was a mix of smooth and bumpy. I sucked on him, and he groaned.

Ty held my cheeks as he fucked my face, while Arik and Drake worked me up to an earth-shattering orgasm. Even more intense now that I was bonded with all three of them.

My release started a cascade effect, and all of my snake demons came inside me, filling me with their cum.

When Ty released my mouth, I slumped forward onto Arik's broad chest. The big demon rumbled. "You better not be tired yet. We're not done with you."

Right. Dick number two for round two.

"I just need to rest for, like, one second." Having every hole filled up was truly exhausting and exhilarating at the same time. But I wanted more, and more, of them—with them.

Drake plucked me from Arik, kissed me with toe-curling passion, then deposited me in Ty's arms as he went to the bathroom to clean up. Ty cradled me against his chest. I sighed, content.

"Let's decorate her," Drake said as he returned, blue eyes gleaming.

I glanced from Ty to Arik, then back to Drake, trying to figure out exactly what he meant by that. None of them cared to explain. The only clue I got was Ty easing me down on my back and ordering me to stay put.

Their spent dicks disappeared and were replaced by erect ones. I stayed where I was as the three of them surrounded me, on their knees, cocks in hand. Arik and Ty fondled my breasts, and Drake's skillful fingers pumped into my pussy.

"Make yourself come," Drake ordered.

I licked my lips, watching them stroke their thick cocks. Sliding my hands down my body, I did as I was told and played with my clit. Their grunts and moans were holiday carols to my ears. The sounds of their pleasure heightened my own arousal.

I cried out as I came, and a moment later ropes of hot cum splattered on my skin. They painted me, until my stomach, chest, and face were covered in white. Like icing on a cake.

Three pairs of slitted eyes gazed appreciatively down at me for a long moment.

Breaking the spell, Drake kissed my nose. "Happy Yule, love."

I beamed up at them. My snake demons. My fated mates. My forevers.

"Happy Yule. I love you. All of you." My tone held the same conviction I felt in my heart.

Their features softened, their eyes sparkled.

"I love you too." Drake kissed my mouth this time.

Arik stole the next kiss. "You have my heart, gorgeous."

Ty swooped in and plucked me from Arik's arms. His dark gaze serious, he said, "You have my heart and my soul, princess. Forever and always."

My insides fluttered. I felt so light and airy that I would float away on a bubble of happiness.

I claimed his mouth. "Now let's go hang those ornaments you made on the Yule tree in the Dean's Hall, find some more cookies, and drink peppermint cocoa in front of the hearth." I bounced out of bed, giddy.

This was going to be a lovely day, followed by a wonderful New Year. And a fantastic life.

Thank you for reading *Venomous Tidings*! If you enjoyed this bit of holiday fun, please leave a review. Reviews are like tips for authors, and I'd greatly appreciate it!

Want more of this magical academy world? Read the completed **Academy Obscura** series.

THE FLAME WITHIN - BLURB

When her hidden flame ignites, she'll change the supernatural world forever.

I didn't know paranormal creatures existed until I'm forced to enroll at Academy Obscura, the mandatory two year college for everyone with magical powers.

Except I don't have any of those special powers.

And that's a real problem, because the students who fail their classes join the Culling. That doesn't mean I'll get to leave. Nope. It means I'll be sacrificed to soul-eating creatures to keep an ancient truce alive.

I supposedly come from a long line of royal witches, and my professors are determined to prove it's true.

Jaxon's my witch professor who thinks he can threaten my powers into existence. Liam, the alluring Fae, awakens something in me, but I don't think it's magic. My broody wolf shifter professor, Angel, ignores the sparks flying between us.

I don't belong here, but there seems to be only two ways out. Give up and die, or find the magic within myself before it's too late.

THE FLAME WITHIN

CHAPTER ONE
CAPRICE

I was driving fast up the freeway, probably too fast, but it was an evening for speed. The summer between high school and college was supposed to be filled with adventure and recklessness. These were the best days of our lives, after all.

Elena sat in the passenger seat, bright red bikini top showing off her perfect tan. Her long, wavy black hair was twisted into a messy bun.

She cranked up the radio. "Love this song!" Elena started to sing along. She was so tone deaf. I laughed, drumming on the steering wheel.

The last rays of sunlight shone through the driver side window, and I shifted the visor to block it out.

My tan arms were showing a faint pinkish hue from the day spent at the beach.

"This summer is the best. And this party is going to be epic," Elena said.

I glanced at her over the top of my sunglasses. We were on our way to crash a University of Maryland Baltimore County party. Both of us would be attending UMBC in the fall. May as well check out their party life now.

I smiled, never sure which one of us was the bad influence over the other. Maybe it didn't matter. Since we met each other sophomore year of high school, we'd been inseparable.

Changing lanes, I zoomed around several cars in a row.

We arrived at the beach, parked, and grabbed our tote bags. Opening the car door, the warm, humid air blasted me. Instantly coating my skin with a sheen of sweat.

The sun was setting in the hills behind us. The beach swarmed with college students in shorts and tank tops. At one end was a volleyball net, at the other some tables set up with a row of kegs. In the middle of the sand, the bonfire was about to be lit.

I glanced at Elena. "What you think?"

"Let's start with beer."

We marched over to the kegs and poured ourselves a couple of drinks. I turned around to survey the crowd. Someone had turned up the music and people started to dance in the sand. The hip-hop beat thumped along with my pulse.

"Hey, lovelies." The guy approaching us was buff and tan. His blond hair cut short. He smiled, showing perfect white teeth. Damn, I didn't realize such hotties went to UMBC. He was probably a jerk, most hot guys were.

"Heyyy…" Elena said. She was totally checking him out.

He cozied up to her. "Wanna dance?" He took her hand and led her out to the unofficial dance floor.

I sipped the beer, watching them for a while as the last rays of light disappeared. Chewing on the inside of my cheek, I was unsure of what to do. I could go dance by myself. Or hang out on the side and people-watch.

From across the bonfire, a guy caught my eye. He was wearing sunglasses, which I thought was weird now that the sun had gone down. Even though I couldn't see his eyes, I knew he was looking at me, I could sense it. A shiver ran down my arms.

He moved slowly in my direction. Not directly. He skirted the perimeter of the party, eventually ending up about ten feet from me. He stood in the shadows, just out of reach of the bonfire's light.

I blinked and he vanished. Something about him captured my full attention. More than anything, I wanted to find him, to see him again. I couldn't explain this sudden, overwhelming curiosity.

Intrigued, I approached where I'd last seen him

standing. Maybe he'd gone around the side of the restroom building. I circled it. He wasn't anywhere around, yet I thought I could feel his presence. Or at least, it felt like someone was watching me.

Then he appeared behind me. I spun around. He'd taken off the sunglasses. In the dim light, I could make out a defined jawline, broad shoulders, and short dark hair.

He stood so close that I could smell him. A heady scent of fresh spring water and pine.

I swayed toward him. Alarm bells went off in the back of my brain. Something wasn't right about him.

"Look at me." His voice was deep, rich, and compelling.

My eyes lifted to his, which seemed to glow with a faint silver light. I couldn't look away.

"I'm going to kiss you," he said.

I continued to stare up at him, unable to say anything or move. We were in the dark, behind the restrooms where no one could see us.

He grabbed my waist and lifted, stepping forward until I was pinned between him and the concrete wall. All the while, he still held my gaze. His hands slid up from my waist to brush against my breasts, but they didn't linger there. They continued up to palm either side of my face. He licked his lips, then brought his mouth to mine.

His lips were warm and soft, yet demanding. He deepened the kiss. Parting my lips with his tongue.

I felt dizzy, like I'd had too much to drink. But my

half consumed beer was still clutched in my hand. It was like this guy had some power over me. Or I was in a dream. None of it seemed real.

The floaty feeling lessened when I noticed his hands had returned to my body. One hand was wrapped around my waist while the other cupped my bikini-encased breast. The warmth of his hand seeped through the thin fabric. He caught my nipple between two fingers. I gasped.

The shock jolted me back to reality. What was I doing? I didn't even know this guy. And I didn't want to be this easy. I'd had sex once. Years ago. My second time was not going to be behind a bathroom with a stranger.

I dropped the beer cup, freeing up my hands to push against his solid chest.

He drew back and locked his gaze on mine. "You will not resist me."

The weird light-headed feeling came back. My body went limp in his arms, and he lowered us to the sun-warmed sand. He leered down at my scantily clad body. That silver glow flaring in his eyes.

When his weight pressed down on me, something snapped alert in my brain again.

I shoved at him with all my strength. He seemed unprepared for it and rolled to the side. I took the opportunity to jump up and run. Twenty feet away, the party was in full swing.

Panicked, I sped through the crowd trying to find Elena. The music was blasting so loud that I couldn't hear anything over it. In the middle, I circled. I didn't see Elena, but the creepy guy was lurking on the outside, his gaze fixed on me. Like a predator waiting for his prey.

Blood rushed in my ears as I spun again, searching for Elena. A million horrible questions popped into my head. How was I going to get out of here? Was the guy Elena danced with a freak too? Had he taken her somewhere?

Then I spotted her. She was with the same blond guy. They were making out by the volleyball net.

I pushed through the twerking bodies to the other side. At a dead run, I closed the distance between me and my friend. Without a word, I grabbed her arm, pulling her toward the car.

"What the hell?" Elena said, struggling to free herself.

"We need to leave. Right now. Questions later." I'd lost my tote, but I didn't care. The car keys were in my shorts pocket. I fished them out. Dropped them on the asphalt. Then picked them up with shaking hands.

"Seriously, what's going on?" Elena wrenched her arm out of my grip.

I faced her. "Get in the car."

Whatever expression I wore must have scared her. Her face paled, and she sprinted around to the passenger side.

I pressed the fob to unlock the car. Just as I reached for the handle, the creep appeared right behind Elena. I screamed.

He spun her around to face him. "Sleep," he commanded.

She fell to the ground. What the hell?

His eyes locked on me. "No human can resist me. Few others can either. What are you?"

I didn't know what he was talking about. His words barely registered. I needed to get Elena and myself out of there. But she lay on the other side of the car at his feet.

The blond that Elena had been making out with approached us. "What's going on here?" he asked.

I stepped closer to him "Help. This creep…he did something to her. He's trying to assault me."

The creep spoke. "She's resisting my compulsion, which is impossible. Be careful. She's not human. I don't know what she is."

Wait. These two knew each other? I moved toward the driver's door.

Blond dude chuckled. "Man, you need to learn the art of subtlety. Now leave them alone." When creep didn't move, Elena's guy said, "Leave. Now." His voice came out strong, almost booming. It was unnatural and freaky as hell.

Creep cursed, but left. The blond strode over to where Elena lay unconscious. He picked her up, opened the car door, and buckled her into the passenger seat. With a glance at me, he said, "Sorry about that. My friend gets a little carried away."

I didn't care what his excuse was. I started the car,

slamming my door shut. As soon as the passenger door closed, I sped out of the parking lot.

I glanced at Elena. She still slept. At least, I hoped she was just sleeping.

My heart was pounding too fast. My hands shook on the steering wheel. That creep had done something to my brain. Like some kind of mind game. Hypnotism, or something. I'd almost given into him. Almost. A chill radiated from my chest. I shivered.

I turned on the radio. The music helped, as I took deep breaths in and out. When I was feeling more stable, I reached over to shake Elena's shoulder. Her eyelids fluttered open. She sat up.

"What's going on?" she asked. "Was I just sleeping?"

I was so relieved she was okay. "Some creep attacked me. Then he went after you, used some kind of hypnotism to make you fall asleep. But that guy you were making out with made the creep go away." That was the best I could sum it up.

"Oh my God, are you all right?" Elena asked, then she cringed. "My head feels foggy."

Frowning, I nodded. "Let's get home."

CHAPTER TWO
CAPRICE

After dropping off Elena at her parent's house, I drove the block and a half to mine, and parked the old Jetta on the street. There were no sidewalks in our neighborhood, so the lawn came right up to the street.

I sat in the car for a few moments to let my heartbeat settle before facing my foster parents. Trying again to wrap my brain around what had happened tonight, it was no use. Hypnotism? Glowing eyes? None of it made any sense.

With a long exhale, I got out of the car and I let myself into the house. Antonio, my foster dad, was up late playing Xbox with my foster brother in the living room. My greeting went unnoticed by them.

Vanessa was in the kitchen cleaning up after dinner. "Hey, sweetie, how was the beach?" She kissed my cheek. As foster parents went, and I had a lot of experience, these two were the best.

"Okay." I'd told her that we were staying out late with a couple of other friends. Not mentioning anything about a frat party or underage drinking.

She finished loading the dishwasher. "Just okay?"

"Yeah. I have a headache, actually." I turned toward the stairs.

"Wait." Vanessa retrieved an envelope from the counter. "You have a letter."

Probably more college information. I took the envelope from her and glanced at the handwritten addresses. It was an elegant cursive, unlike anything I'd ever seen. Who would be writing to me?

Heading up the stairs to my room, I stopped in the doorway. Even after two years here the room didn't really feel like *mine.* That was no fault of Vanessa's, she'd bought the emerald green comforter just for me. Let me put band posters on my walls. And hang strands of clear lights around the window.

But who knew how many foster kids had lived in it before me. And once I left, another one would come in. In six short weeks, I'd leave all of this behind and move into the dorms at UMBC. No more parents, no more of living in other people's houses.

Though, I would stay in touch with Antonio and Vanessa, at least that was my hope. Even though I was already eighteen and free of the system, moving out was the last step.

While I was excited for the changes, a part of me wanted to stand still, to have this summer last a little bit longer. I was ready to not be a kid anymore, but unsure of whether I was ready to become an adult. To really be on my own. Especially if creeps like the one tonight were waiting for me in college.

At least Elena was coming with me. We'd have each other. Watch each others backs.

I closed the door, leaning against it, and lifted the envelope, studying the unfamiliar handwriting once more before ripping it open. Inside was a letter in the same flourished script.

Dear Caprice,

I hope this letter finds you in good health and happiness. My name is Isabella Sorrentino, and I'm your grandmother; your birth father's mother. I have been searching for years to find you, and am so glad that I finally have.

I would love to meet you. Given my age, travel does not agree with me very well. I live in Oregon and I want to pay for a plane ticket for you, so that you may visit me this summer.

My phone number is written at the bottom. Please call me and I will arrange everything. I so look forward to meeting you and telling you about your family.

All my blessings,
Isabella

My head swam, and I crouched down so that I wouldn't fall over. I had blood relatives—or at least one. A grandma.

I stared at the carpet. My heart pounded, filling my ears with its uptempo beat. Tears moistened my cheeks, and I let them fall. I'd dreamed of this letter for years, mostly when I was younger and filled with hope. But it never came—until now.

Wiping the tears away, I reread the letter. What if she had the wrong Caprice Sorrentino? There was a chance that this was all a mistake and I wasn't the granddaughter she sought. It was never good to be too hopeful.

I read it a third time before folding the letter and setting in on my nightstand.

It was late here, but earlier in Oregon. I pulled out my phone and it lit up with a touch. Almost midnight here, which made it nearly nine in the west. I dialed the number that was written as a post script.

It rang four times, and I chewed the inside of my cheek.

"Good evening, this is Isabella." The woman who answered had a deep, purring voice. She had to be old, to be my grandmother, but she didn't sound old.

I cleared my throat. "Hello, Isabella, this is Caprice. I got your letter."

I told Antonio and Vanessa about the letter and phone call at breakfast the next morning. My foster brother Max was the first one to respond.

"So sometimes families do search for their kids?" he asked.

I didn't want to give him too much hope. As far as I knew his dad was in jail and his mom was an addict. He might have a grandparent looking for him, but chances of that were not great.

With a brief smile, I said, "Sometimes."

Vanessa reached over and squeezed my hand. "You may be eighteen, but you're still under our protection. Before you make any plans, I want to make sure this woman is who she says she is."

I nodded. Fair enough.

"I'll call in a favor and have her checked out." Antonio was a lawyer in the District Attorney's office. "If she's really your grandmother, we'll decide what to do next. Together."

Part of me wanted to tell them that I had this all under control, that I'd already made my plans, and could take care of myself. Two years ago I would have done just that. But this family had changed me. They'd made me realize that I didn't have to do everything myself and that I could trust others—or at least these two and Elena.

Trusting three people in the entire world, that was some serious progress.

Antonio went to work and Vanessa packed up Max for summer camp. I lounged on the couch, thumbing through social media but not really absorbing any of it.

It had ended up being a long talk with Isabella last night. My impression was that she was kind, outgoing, and genuinely interested in knowing me. We made tentative plans for August. She told me the sooner she could book the plane ticket the better. But I'd had to talk with my foster parents first, which she totally understood.

My stomach felt light and bubbly, like it was trying to rise up through my throat and float away. I still couldn't believe that I had a grandma and she wanted to meet me. In one night my whole life had changed.

I pushed down on the sensation that I recognized

as hope and excitement. Take it one day at a time. Don't get too consumed by it all. I needed a distraction. I needed to tell Elena.

After a quick text exchange, I got dressed and walked the short distance to Elena's house. I let myself in. Waving to her parents, I jogged up the stairs to her bedroom.

She was an only child, so she had everything. Her room was the epitome of girly-girl decorated in white and pink. It was like living inside a barbie house. Too many frills for me.

For the first time it occurred to me that leaving to live in the dorms was probably going to be harder for her than me. She'd lived here her entire life. What an experience that would be.

"So what's up? Tell me." She sat on her bed, and I joined her.

"This." I handed over the letter.

She read it. Her eyes growing wide. She smiled. "This is great news! I'm so happy for you. I just can't believe it's taken this long."

"I know. I'm still trying to get my head around it." Taking the letter back, I read it again. "What do you think I should do?"

"Is that even a question?" Elena looked at me like I was crazy.

"I guess not. It's just—" I sighed, bringing my legs up and crossing them. "I don't want to be disappointed. What if she's wrong and I'm not her granddaughter?"

"I'm sure she's done lots of research. She had to have gotten your records in order to find you. How many other Caprice Sorrentino's can there be? With your date and place of birth, and who're in the foster system? Like none."

"Right."

Elena threw a pillow at me. "Come on, this is so exciting!"

I smiled. "You're so my cheerleader." Though the words were sarcastic, Elena always encouraged me when I needed it most.

A frown crossed over her delicate Italian features. "What happened last night? At that party? I mean, you told me some, but…what happened?"

I slid the letter into my back pocket. "That guy tried to rape me."

"Oh my God, are you all right?" Elena reached out to take my hand. "We should report him. Call the cops."

I shook my head. "I didn't even get a good look at him. I'd only be able to give them a vague description. And I'm fine. He didn't hurt me. Just freaked me out." For some reason I couldn't explain, I didn't want to go into the details of the mind control and glowing eyes. Plus, he'd said I wasn't human. How freaky was that? My chest clenched. I pushed the familiar feeling of panic back down. Why were his words bringing up this old anxiety?

I shrugged off the feeling. "I think we should be

more careful, though. Last night…I feel like I was lucky that it didn't turn out worse."

"Yeah, I totally agree. From now on, we stick together at parties."

"Deal."

"Want to get out of here?" Elena asked.

"Sure." We spent another long day at the beach. The warmth and relaxation helped me to almost forget about last night. It was hard to imagine predators even existing on such a perfect day.

I returned home late. Antonio was waiting up for me in the living room. He motioned for me to come sit on the couch. It was after ten o'clock and Vanessa had already turned in.

I sat down. "What's up?"

"I have some good news for you."

My heart squeezed. I waited for him to continue.

"I looked into your grandma. Her name is Isabella Sorrentino and she is the late Luca Sorrentino's mother. She lives in Estacada, Oregon, which is right outside of Portland. Before she retired, she had a long career as a nurse."

Since it was my grandmother contacting me, I'd figured my birth father was either dead or in jail. Still, the shock of knowing he was gone made my stomach drop.

"So she's legit?" I asked.

"You have the same last name. I know your father's not listed on your birth certificate, so we can't be one hundred percent positive. But, I did see Luca Sorrentino's drivers license picture, and there's no overlooking the family resemblance."

I swallowed the lump wedged in my throat. "Can I go see her?"

Antonio nodded. "Of course you can. But I don't want you to be in her debt, in case anything…happens. So I bought you a plane ticket. You're leaving the first week in August."

I leaned into him and gave him a bearhug. "Thank you! That means so much to me."

He returned the hug, then pulled away. From his suit coat pocket, he pulled out the printed plane ticket information. "Don't lose this." He handed it to me.

"Thank you. Although, I'll pay you back for it some day."

"Don't worry about it, Caprice. Consider it a graduation present. I know that's hard for you, but just accept it. All right?"

"Okay." I stood. "Thanks again. Goodnight." I went upstairs. A mix of excitement and fear swirled in my gut. I really had a grandma. What if she didn't like me?

August was only a couple of weeks away, I needed to think about packing. And what to wear that would make a good impression. I'd ask Elena, she was always much better at that kind of stuff.

I knew she was still awake, so I sent her a text with the good news. We texted back and forth until two in the morning.

❄

The morning of my trip finally arrived. I was filled with the jitters. Elena was on vacation with her family, and Max was still at summer camp, so only Vanessa and Antonio saw me off at the airport.

With Elena's help, I was all packed. She'd made me borrow a couple of her more conservative dresses, just in case grandma was old-fashioned. I was also required to pack a sweater. Apparently it could get cold in Oregon, even in August. I didn't believe that. But whatever.

"Remember," Antonio said, "when you're ready to come home, you call the airlines and set a return date. If you need to come home sooner than that, just call me."

I nodded.

"And check in every Sunday. Just send me or Vanessa a text. Okay?"

I rolled my eyes. "I am an adult, you know."

"I know. But humor me until you're in college."

I hugged him and Vanessa goodbye.

The flight was long. So long. I didn't know it was possible to stay in the air that many hours. We had one short stopover in Denver. Then the plane continued onto Portland, Oregon.

Between Denver and Portland I dozed. The dream snippet was a familiar one—recurring for at least the past several years. I was in a dark room with dirty brown carpet. It was nighttime. The shouting started from downstairs. "Clumsy bitch! Deserves the belt!" Panicked, I ran down the hall to the stairs. In the living room, tears streamed down the face of a little girl. Everything exploded in red.

I jolted awake in the airplane seat. Always the same dream. But what did it mean?

"We'll be landing in Portland, Oregon in twenty minutes." A voice came through the cabin speakers.

When we landed, of course, my sense of time was all messed up. My internal clock said it was ten at night, but the local time was only seven. It was bright and sunny outside, with a temperature of seventy-nine degrees. At least that's what the flight attendant said as we taxied in.

I grabbed my carry-on once the plane had stopped rolling, then shuffled out with the rest of the people. My grandma had said someone would meet me at the gate and drive me to her house. Apparently, Estacada was about forty minutes from the airport.

As I exited the secured section, I searched around for whoever Isabella had sent. She hadn't told me anything about how I was supposed to recognize them.

I scanned the crowd that waited for their loved ones. My gaze fell on the cardboard sign first. It read: Sorrentino. Then my eyes traveled upward to take in a well-built chest, broad shoulders, a square jaw, and piercing grey eyes under wavy blond hair.

Maybe he was here for a different Sorrentino. Because grandma couldn't possibly be associated with a hunk like that, could she?

The man approached. He was a little older than me, my guess was early twenties.

"Caprice Sorrentino?" he asked. My heart fluttered as he said my name.

I cleared my throat. "Yeah. I'm Caprice."

He smiled, extending his hand. "Jaxon McIver." His hand was warm, dry, and strong. I blushed as I shook it, hoping he wouldn't notice my reaction to him. "Welcome to Oregon, Caprice."

Read the rest here:
https://books2read.com/theflamewithin

SUGGESTED READING ORDER

ACADEMY OBSCURA SERIES

Her Forbidden Fae

The Flame Within

The Fiery Shifter

The Searing Trials

The Scorched Summer

VENOMOUS TIDINGS

HER WICKED MATES SERIES

Captive Beauty

Beastly Desires

Brazen Hearts

Twisted Fates

THREE WICKED BEARS